Flight Path & Other Stories

Jan Bowman

Evening Street Press

Dublin, Ohio

Evening Street Press

October 2015

Dublin, Ohio

Names, characters, events are the product of the author's imagination and bear no resemblance to actual events or persons, living or dead.

All rights revert to the author on publication
© Copyright 2015 by Evening Street Press.

ISBN: 978-1-937347-29-1
Printed in the United States of America

Evening Street Press
625 Edgecliff Dr
Columbus, OH 43235
www.eveningstreetpress.com

For All Of Us - as we seek kindness as the only thing that makes sense anymore.

To Jeanne with gratitude

FLIGHT PATH & Other Stories

Table of Contents

Mermaids	1
Skating Blind	12
Flight Path	17
After Life	32
Wait on Me	45
Rabbits	55
Kindness	63
Unnatural Disasters	77
This Arrow Marks Me	82
After the Rain	89
Acknowledgments	108

MERMAIDS

When I was twelve I learned about mermaids from my sixteen-year-old cousin Danny, who was staying at our beach house on the coast of Delaware with his mother, my aunt Nora, the summer my parents' marriage fell apart. He waved a *Playboy* magazine in my face and showed me pictures of beautiful women in silver gossamer tops. "Mermaids," he assured me, and grinned knowingly at photographs of two women resting on a large rock, combing each other's long flowing hair. "Too bad you'll never look like them." He snickered and flipped through the pages. "Emily, how does it feel to be skinny and flat-chested like a guy?"

"Let me see," I said, and grabbed the magazine, and then stared in awe at a page of photographs. Beautiful women embraced under the title "Mermaids of the Atlantic." They seemed to drift in shallow water along the tide line. Scales on their rainbow-colored tails shimmered as they curled against each other amid rocks, sand, and pink shells. Their faces were in shadows, but their graceful necks were like those of swans I had seen at the park near my house in Baltimore.

"Don't tell anybody I showed you this." He gave me a menacing look.

I shrugged and feigned no interest. I hated the way Danny treated me. "Those women aren't real, Danny. It's all faked with makeup and feathers."

"Who cares? They're sexy." He seized the magazine, folded it and tucked it into the back pocket of his jeans, and retreated to his room.

That summer I became a proficient swimmer, astonished by the growing strength of my scrawny arms and legs as they propelled me through the cold, uneven waves off the shore. Although my mother had forbidden me to swim alone in the ocean, I swam daily, not in the nearby pool, as she supposed, but in the surf about a mile down the shore from our house. My mother was too preoccupied to notice how I spent my afternoons. I plunged into the cool surf and swam against heavy waves. I practiced slipping into the sea from sunny rocks.

Afterward, I lay on warm concrete bulkheads and imagined myself with a sleek, glistening tail. The pictures from the magazine lingered in my thoughts as I wandered the beach at sunrise and sunset, straining my eyes for a glimmer of a mermaid's scales. My dreams took on a new vitality that later I realized was the nucleus of desire.

In the late afternoons, I walked along the shore and measured my distance from home by the flagpole in front of our beach house. The house rippled in lines of heat from the sun, and from a great way off the house seemed to float castle-like above the sand. My father had inherited the beachfront property years earlier from his uncle.

At one time, the two-story pink house had hunched over sand dunes three streets from the tide line. Several decades of fall hurricanes had sucked two rows of oceanfront houses into the sea, leaving the bulk of my father's legacy listing on stilted legs, like a roseate ibis, leaning into the wind. The closer one drew to it, the more the house seemed to stumble and catch itself at the ocean's edge.

Waves lapped against the pilings under the ocean side of the house at high tide. In the light of the full moon, the screened porch creaked as whirling waters tugged at the house, whispering seductively, testing the tenacity of the sloping floorboards. Summer evenings I sat on the floor stroking the cool wood planks with my hands, tantalized by the hazards of splinters. With no one my age to amuse me, I listened to the mutterings of the house and watched the waves, vaguely aware of a dull, prodding unease I supposed was loneliness. Sometimes my mother played cards with me. The television, broken the previous summer, remained dusty and ignored. My mother preferred the silence.

She was tall, blond, willowy, and increasingly remote when my father was around. That summer she developed dark circles of worry around her eyes. I heard her sometimes walking about the unlit house late at night, banging into furniture, crying out softly. She sat each morning drinking coffee on the screened porch, her hands tightening around the cup as she watched the ocean's daily attacks on the underpinnings of our house.

My father, a criminal court judge, stayed in Baltimore during the week and came out only on weekends, a visitor in his own home. He arrived most Friday nights around eight, splendidly pressed in a white shirt and dark suit in spite of the heat. "Muriel, my scotch," he would say, ordering a triple Chivas on the rocks with a twist, with a wave of his hand, as if he were in a familiar restaurant. My mother always rushed to accommodate his request, as though she had not anticipated it.

He rarely spoke to me except to inquire whether I was reading books from the summer list he'd posted on the refrigerator and which included two of his favorites: *Tom Sawyer* and *Huck Finn*. I lied that I was. Perhaps he knew his simple inquiry would lead me to a hasty retreat before he could question me.

He liked politics and had begun to talk about running for governor. He did not seem to like being at the beach. He never went swimming, and only once do I remember him walking on the beach with my mother. Even then, he wore his suit and hard black shoes, and only removed his tie. Most of the time, he sat on the screened porch smoking, sipping scotch and reading court briefs. In the evenings, after dinner he and my mother argued quietly behind the closed door of her bedroom while I worried about our family.

Sunday afternoons the house seemed to exhale with relief when at three o'clock he shoved papers into a black leather valise and left. He backed his Lincoln out of the driveway without so much as a wave. I imagined him speeding across the toll bridge to the city, pursued by my mother's unhappiness.

In July of that summer, my mother invited her sisters to the beach house as a buffer for my father's visits. Nora and Clarissa were older, less elegant versions of my mother. The sisters had always been close. During the week, they played tennis, sang silly songs, shopped, played cards, and started the cocktail hour around four every afternoon. My mother's spirits improved once her sisters arrived. She talked about painting again and her eyes grew bright and filled with conviction until the weekend arrived.

I eavesdropped on whispered conversations she had with my aunts and learned more about her sadness. "Morgan doesn't care anymore." I heard the break in my mother's voice as she told them, "I think we're headed for a divorce, but please don't tell Emily, not yet." And so I knew, and wished every day that I did not.

My aunts eased the tensions. Both had majored in literature. Clarissa, the oldest, a literature professor, was reliable and solid, although my father said, "She drinks vats of gin and stares at the tides too long, and she quotes all that damned poetry."

One of Clarissa's favorites was Emily Dickinson: *"I do not doubt the self I was; was Competent to me. But something awkward in the fit proves that outgrown I see."* To which my mother would reply, "Clarissa, you still make the trains run on time, in spite of your fondness for gin." As a child I thought Clarissa worked for a railroad.

Nora, four years younger than Clarissa, sang off-color songs and quoted long literary passages that weren't particularly funny to me, but happily they made my mother laugh. Nora worked with a theater group. Often at dinner she recited bawdy passages from Shakespeare in her best theatrical voice while Danny studied water spots on his silverware.

Nora told my mother that I was an "aftershock of salaciousness on a summer afternoon." Later, after I had found the word *salacious* in the dictionary, I felt vaguely embarrassed. I could not imagine my father salacious for even a moment in his life.

My aunts' husbands had escaped their marriages in different ways. Clarissa's husband, Rob, was a workaholic lawyer, and though they remained married in name and finances, they rarely saw each other. Nora had divorced Uncle Cal five years earlier, after she caught him with Danny's babysitter. Danny was Nora's only attempt at motherhood. She acknowledged his presence reluctantly. Danny bullied me and made jokes about us all behind our backs. He was not inclined to get a summer job and since he had nowhere else to go, he hung out on the beach and at the fishing docks. He and his buddies spent their days leering at girls who walked along the beach. In the evenings they bathed themselves in cologne and swaggered off to play miniature golf.

The week after Danny showed me the pictures, I slipped into his room and found his collection of *Playboy* magazines under his mattress. The one with the mermaid pictures was on the top of the stack. I hid the magazine in my room, and after lunch I opened it and stared at "Mermaids of the Atlantic."

Much to my surprise, the magazine had pages of naked women lying about in various positions. Feeling strangely lightheaded, I traced the outline of exposed breasts and hips with my fingers. I took off my warm, wet bathing suit and stared at my body in the mirror. My breasts were small. I did not look like the women in the magazine at all.

I studied the pictures, reading captions under the photographs, as words like *erotic* and *sappho* washed over me. My pulse raced with the solid, rapid strokes of an ardent swimmer. I slipped back into my swimsuit, pulled a shirt over it, and tiptoed into the hall. I located Nora's *Dictionary of Myths and Legends* next to the Scrabble board in the bookcase behind the stairs. I slipped it under my shirt and walked softly back to my room.

I could not find some of the words at first, but I found *mermaids* and read, *"According to legend, a mermaid never comes to a false heart."* I looked back at the magazine photographs. The pictures left me trembling and weak.

When I heard my mother's footsteps in the hallway, I closed the dictionary and slipped the magazine under a towel just as my mother opened the door.

"Emily, honey, you're awfully quiet in here," she said. "Oh, you're reading. I thought perhaps you were taking a nap." She studied my sweating face and glanced at the dictionary. "What an odd thing to read," she said as she swirled a martini in a frosty glass.

She looked as if she'd been crying. "Will you ride your bike down to the fishing pier and get some shrimp for dinner tonight?" She stood in the doorway. "Your father hates shrimp, but he's not coming this weekend." She stared at me closely, appraising my loyalty. "He's working on a major case."

Later, after I bought the shrimp at the store, I pushed my bike along the sandy road home. Thick, salty storm clouds spun their way across the bay and rumbled inland. The pain in my mother's eyes when she mentioned my father made my throat hurt. I got on the bike and pedaled violently just as huge raindrops spattered the sand into pockmarked grids, splashing over the double plastic bags of shrimp. I didn't want to go home; I wanted to ride in the rain forever.

I dropped the bike beside the back door and took the drippy bags into the kitchen. Nora stood at the sink, mixing a large pitcher of martinis. Brine from the leaking bags of icy shrimp formed a puddle at my feet, but she was pleasantly oblivious as she waved me toward the sink. "Glad you're back," she said. "I was just about to send Danny out to look for you."

Danny sat sullenly at the kitchen table removing pickles from a tuna sandwich.

"You've been in my room, you little runt," he said, glaring at me fiercely. He turned to Nora. "Tell her to stay out of my stuff."

"Danny, your room is such a mess, I can't imagine anyone going in there for any reason," Nora said.

Danny's ears turned red. He stuffed the sandwich in his mouth and shrugged.

I avoided looking at him, wiped off with a kitchen towel, and hurried upstairs. Danny had ransacked my room, but he had not found the magazine hidden in the back of my closet. I locked the closet door, tied the key around my neck with a string, and retreated to the porch to watch the rain that had settled in for the evening. The smell of shrimp steaming in beer in the kitchen filled the house. I felt almost unbearably sad.

After dinner, Danny left to hang out with his friends while my aunts and my mother argued over their card game well into the night. I fell asleep with the mermaid magazine and dreamed of the women I had seen in the photographs.

The next afternoon I paddled our dinghy out beyond the waves and studied the rocky coastline with binoculars. Elation washed over me. Mermaids were sunning themselves just as I had expected, on a rocky outcropping near a wild section of the beach. Rowing and swimming into the area seemed impossible, what with riptides surging. The surf was unsafe for even an experienced swimmer. After dragging the dinghy ashore into a cove farther up the rocky beach, I hiked the two miles down the rough shoreline, climbed over the dunes and down an embankment to the cove. I shaded my eyes against the sun.

Mermaids, I thought, until I moved closer and saw that they had feet and legs, and hips. Three women lay spread out on blankets on smooth rocks below. At first I wondered if my mother and aunts had discovered the cove, but all of these women had dark hair and they were completely naked. Their bodies were wonderfully tan, like the women I had seen in the magazine. Their bathing suits were stretched beside them on the sand.

I sat down in the shadows, a trembling voyeur, as waves plunged over the rocks and sent up walls of spray. Their voices, carried by the breeze, tinkled like wind chimes.

As the sun dipped low in the sky, the women gathered their things. The smell of coconut suntan lotion mixed with strawberry fragrance, drifted through the air. I slipped away and walked the two miles back to the dinghy on unsteady legs.

I returned the next afternoon and the next. On the third afternoon, three bathing suits lay on the rocks, but only two women sat on beach towels, their arms around each other, staring out at the waves. The third was nowhere to be seen. All at once, someone reached around the outcropping of rock where I crouched and grabbed me.

"I've got him," said the woman as she spun me around to face her. "Spying on us, you little jerk." Her fingers dug into my shoulder. I burst into tears.

The woman dropped her hands to her side and stared. "It's a girl." The other two women leapt over the rocks and ran to us. The three women surrounded me.

"Watching us, are you," said my captor. "You know, that's really rude."

"Oh, she's just a baby," said one of the women. "Cute. But I'd bet she's not even twelve."

"She's too young," said the one who had captured me. She leaned forward and looked at my face carefully. "Give her ten years. What's your name, kid?"

I was embarrassed and yet thrilled to find myself so close to these women. I felt like a specimen pressed under glass. "Emily," I said, smoothing the rocky sand with my bare foot to avoid looking directly at their bodies.

"Have you told anybody about us, Emily?"

"No," I said, relieved that I had not yielded to an earlier urge to impress Danny with my discovery.

"Look at her," said the tall woman, lifting her sunglasses. "She hasn't a clue, do you, sweetie?" She patted me on the head. "Emily, do us a favor and don't mention this to anyone, okay?"

I nodded. Off in the distance, storm clouds rumbled along the horizon. "I have to get home. They'll be looking for me," I lied.

Inhibited by the women's sensuality and kindness, I willed my wobbly legs into motion. I looked over my shoulder twice as I climbed the rocks out of the cove. They were putting on their swimsuits. Later, I would regret that I had not waved.

Twice that week I returned, but the women were not there. I awoke in the night breathing hard, as though I had swum a great distance. During the day I walked the beach, numbly aware of the growing tension in the house. My mother spent more time alone each day. Her sisters hovered about, worry lining their faces, and they took trays of food to her bedroom when she missed dinner.

Looking back now, I barely trust my memory of the next few weeks, so much happened. My father did not come to the beach house that weekend or the next. Then he telephoned late one Friday afternoon, and I watched Nora raise her eyebrows when he requested that she give his excuse to my mother. Danny, who admired my father more than I did, pulled me aside. "He's got someone on the side, you know," he said. "All men do." He seemed pleased by this, and I felt the thick anger of betrayal building in the back of my throat.

At dinner my mother sat grimly resolved.

My aunts cleared the dishes and left us alone.

"Emily," she said finally, "I need to talk to you." And so, late into the evening we sat in the dark listening to the soft slap of high tide against the porch stairs. "Your father and I are not happy together," she began, and as she told me what I already knew, the house seemed to roll ever so slightly, like a ship anchored in a shallow bay.

I was rendered older in those moments. By the end of it, I felt dizzy and vaguely ill. My mother looked relieved by the telling, as though a great weight had shifted between us. I imagined the house an island. And yet I felt safe knowing my mother could leave my father, but not me.

Later the next day on my way home from a movie, I was surprised to see my father's picture on the front page in late editions of the *Baltimore Sun* on the racks outside the theater. The newspaper carried the shocking headline of my father's arrest in Baltimore for soliciting a prostitute. The paper had used an old photograph of him dressed in what Nora called his Clark Gable look. It was my mother's favorite picture of my father from his Princeton yearbook. And though I was not sure what the headline really meant, I realized, even then, that such a thing brought a shameful end to a judiciary career.

I raced home on my bike and found Nora on the phone talking to a reporter. Her angry voice echoed throughout the house. "No, you may not speak with her," she said. "Stop calling." She hung up the phone and muttered, "The damn vultures are circling."

Clarissa sat blowing her nose into a tissue. "What a disgrace," she said. She shook her head when I asked her what *soliciting* meant. "Where'd you hear that word?" she asked. But she didn't wait for me to answer. She told me that my mother was in her bedroom. "And please don't bother her right now." I went upstairs to my room and heard my mother crying in the bedroom next to it. My aunts moved about the house murmuring, with sturdy drinks in hand. "Nothing shocks me anymore," Nora said. "I thought he was involved with someone, but this is sad." And Clarissa agreed.

I longed to escape the creaking sorrow of that house. As I left to walk along the shore, I found Danny sitting outside on the back stairs. He glanced up at me when I passed. "Guess you know what a prostitute is," he said. "You'd think he could do better than that. You'd think he would have a mistress." He stopped cleaning his nails with a penknife and stood up. "If they think to ask, I'm out." He headed toward the boardwalk.

Walking along the shore, I watched the steady ripples of the incoming tide as a sandpiper scurried along the surf's edge. I sat down in the sand and thought about my parents. I did not know my father at all and my mother only a little. But at that moment comfort came to me in thinking about the mystery and kindness of the women I had seen in the cove. And I felt foolish for even thinking they were mermaids.

Over the years, I have heard a number of versions of that summer. Sometimes I watch this same account in my mind's eye as if it were a movie about unhappy people I barely knew. My father came to talk with my mother the following evening, and he left her room after only a few minutes. I have been told he asked to speak to me, but my aunts sent him away. I saw him from the stairwell as he passed through the house. He did not look like Clark Gable at all. He looked tired and sorrowful. He spoke softly to my aunts as he let himself out.

We did not return to our house in Baltimore. So much happened so fast. My aunts packed our things. We moved to a small town in Florida where my mother began teaching art. And I entered a new school and discovered a name for the mermaids I had seen. The house was sold in the spring and washed into the Atlantic next hurricane season.

I don't remember if I saw my father again that year, although surely I did, but I do remember how he smelled of scotch the few times I did see him. He died in a car accident two years later.

But I clearly remember that on the last bright evening I ever spent at my father's beach house, I walked down to the water's edge. As the ocean roiled at high tide, the moonlight on the water gave an illusion of the mystery of scales and skin and flowing hair moving just below the surface.

SKATING BLIND

Audrey skated near the edge of her driveway over a rough place in concrete flawed by a builder's poor mixture of sand and water. She closed her eyes, rolling blind. Listening. Taking comfort in the sound of her skates and the breeze on her face. The driveway's rough texture was familiar and reassuring, although her knees knew the sudden feel of it. Even with her eyes closed, she knew where she was. Late-afternoon light slipped in under her eyelids. Pumping her legs, she swung her arms for balance and skated faster, away from the heaviness of a late-August Sunday. Tomorrow was her tenth birthday. School started next week and her mother had spent the afternoon baking her favorite chocolate brownie cake. She smelled the warm chocolate as she skated near the house.

The scent from late-summer roses reminded her she was coasting near the garage. Opening one eye slowly, she checked to see how close she was to the stairs near the screened side porch. Tilting her skates inward, she ground to a stop, wiped her face, and sat down to examine an adhesive bandage dangling from her knee. The fresh scrape leaked pale fluid that mixed with dirt and perspiration, leaving a stripe from knee to shin.

She looked up at the sound of a car passing slowly. A black Ford stopped, backed up with a high-pitched whine and the driver eased the car into the driveway. He leaned out the window. He wore an Army cap pulled low in the middle of his head. It was like the one Bill, her older sister Judy's fiancé, wore when he left for Korea in January. For a moment she wondered if Bill had come home early as a surprise for her birthday party tomorrow.

The driver squinted even though the sun was behind him. He opened the door, hesitated before walking up the driveway. His crisp tan uniform had wet crescents under the arms. He took off his cap and glanced at the numbers on their house. The six on their house number leaned a bit until it had almost slipped into a nine position. The other man in the passenger seat nodded, and the driver took a deep breath. He smiled, but only with his lips. "We're looking for the Howell residence. Is your father home?"

Behind Audrey the screen door squeaked as her father opened it, his steps heavy as he crossed the porch. "Hello, I'm Ben Howell. What can I do for you?"

She turned at the sound of her father's strained, clipped tone. His hands gripped the door; she felt his fear. Her skates wobbled underneath her.

The soldier stepped toward her father. "Sergeant Smith," he said. The other man got out of the car and walked across the driveway toward them. "And Captain Taylor from Fort Meade. We tried to call earlier. But your phone seems to be out of order." Grass from the fresh-mowed lawn stuck to their shiny black shoes. Captain Taylor's flat hat, trimmed in gold braid, had a glossy black visor.

Audrey sat down on the warm pavement of the driveway and took off her skates. Her damp socks left footprints on the concrete, which dried quickly in the heat. The radio crackled and was silenced in the middle of the Sunday Evening Serenade. Her mother had switched off the radio. Sheer white curtains in the dining room moved slightly. Her mother was there, almost out of sight, listening.

"This is not a good day for either of us, Mr. Howell," the captain said. His mouth drooped slightly and his chin twitched. "I understand your daughter Judy was engaged to Private William R. Thomas. He named you as the person to contact." The captain blinked. "In the event something happened . . ."

Her father clenched his fists. His eyes searched the surface of the concrete fiercely, as if looking for someone to blame for the flaw in his driveway. He'd had the same expression in January when his mother—Audrey's grandmother, who had lived with them—died.

An image came back to Audrey of the dark mahogany box that smelled sickeningly of flowers as it was lowered into the ground. She closed her eyes against the thought and held her breath. She still had night terrors of roots and rocks crushing the box.

The captain cleared his throat. "Sir, William wanted you to tell your daughter, Judy. And of course, be there when we talk with his mother." He hesitated and his fingers nervously traced the outline of his watch. "I understand your older daughter is away at college?"

Her father nodded. "She's taking extra summer classes to finish early. So they can get married . . ."

The captain shifted his eyes to the roses growing beside the steps. "I understand that his mother is a widow. And as he was her only child, it's likely to be overwhelming. William wanted you to help make decisions to spare his mother as much as possible." Captain Taylor coughed. "He left written instructions. Said you were like the father he never knew."

Audrey's mother stood at the closed screen door with a tissue clasped in her hand. She moaned softly.

"How?" whispered Audrey's father. He sat down on the top step outside the screened porch.

"He was driving a truck. Shelling wiped out a stretch of mountain road on a foggy morning run. His truck slipped off the mountain, flipped over, and crushed him. They got him back to base camp and the surgeons did all they could." The captain folded his hands over his belt buckle and looked away. "His remains should be returned in about two weeks."

Reddish hair around the captain's temples stuck to his forehead. Sweat gathered along his closely cut sideburns. Blond hair on his wrist curled around his metal watchband. His military watch looked exactly like the one Bill wore.

In her mind, Audrey could see Bill's wrists. Even at twenty-one he had no hair on his arms. He had strong hands.

She remembered those hands swinging her up in the air. His slender fingers gave her packages of Juicy Fruit gum. He said, "Don't chew the whole pack of gum at once. You don't want your mother to get mad at me, do you?" He winked at her as he hugged her sister and they danced around the living room. He laughed now inside her head.

Captain Taylor's watery eyes bulged slightly under heavy lids. He was a man with a kind of cold sadness that she'd never seen before. He blinked again and Audrey shivered. "We are so very sorry for your loss."

The sergeant strode to the car and returned carrying a packet of papers tied with flat green string. He handed the packet to the captain.

Audrey's father gripped the door and unsteadily pulled himself to standing. Her mother, waiting in the shadows, held a white tissue against her lips.

"Sir, I am sorry to do this right now, but we have some papers for you to review, as to the arrangements and so forth." Captain Taylor said. He glanced past the shadows into the screened porch toward Audrey's mother. "Do you have a table where we can spread out these documents?"

"Audrey's mother turned on a light and held the screen door open. "Come into the kitchen." As the men filed past her into the house, her father introduced her mother. Audrey slipped in behind them and stood in the doorway.

Audrey's freshly baked chocolate cake cooled on the sideboard in the kitchen.

Her mother looked in the direction of the cake and seemed to see her for the first time. "Oh honey, Bill . . ." She pulled Audrey close and hugged her. "Please go and read or watch television for a while so we can talk." She turned to look at the captain.

In the darkness of the living room, the scent of furniture polish, chocolate cake, and cedar from the nearby closet left Audrey dizzy. For Valentine's Day Bill had sent Judy a box of candy filled with light and dark chocolates in the shapes of skaters in a polished mahogany box lined with purple quilted paper.

Audrey sat on the floor in her favorite spot behind the piano and ran her hands over the smooth dark wood. Judy, Bill, and her grandmother sang at this piano last Christmas. Her ears rang with remembered voices. She ran her fingers over the dust along the baseboard behind the piano. Her hands touched a spider-web. Exhaling slowly, she remembered one of her grandmother's stories about ancient, magical powers of spider-webs. In the old days, before modern cures, people put clumps of webs into wounds to stop bleeding.

Audrey drew her knees up close to her chest. Her ribs ached, as though she had fallen while skating and lost her breath. She pressed her arms tight against her stomach and listened to the murmur of voices coming from the nearby room. She extended her arms and stared at her hands, wondering how it felt to die. She touched her knee and pulled the bandage away. Small drops of blood surfaced on the scrape. Collecting strands of sticky web from behind the piano, she pressed it into the soft brown center of the wound on her knee. Rocking slowly, she blocked out the sounds of her mother sobbing in the kitchen. She closed her eyes, and in her mind she skated, blind with the breeze in her face

FLIGHT PATH

Years ago Anna took them all to Kings Dominion. She remembers stopping the Chevy at the amusement park entrance and her then-fourteen-year-old son Tommy leaping from the car and leaving her to unload her husband Patrick alone. "Wait," she called to him as he raced toward ticket booths and turnstiles. He returned reluctantly as Patrick clawed her neck and shoulder with one of his two prostheses. Balancing himself with his cane, Patrick reached for his backpack with his good hand, and pint bottles of cheap bourbon clinked around in the old worn thing. At ten a.m., the August heat was already merciless. She felt as if she qualified for combat pay.

Anna gave Patrick an envelope with their prepaid two-day admissions passes. "You and Tommy wait here at the gate while I park the car," she told him, shielding her eyes from the sun.

"I can't do much to stop the boy at this point." Patrick looked down at his cane. "He can damn well outrun me. But I guess it won't kill him to wait a few minutes."

Anna handed a tote bag to Tommy. "Hang on to this; it has our camera and sun lotion." Tommy took the bag and swung it in a circle. "Stop doing that," Anna said. "Do you want to break the camera?" This was not the vacation she'd envisioned when the travel agency where she worked awarded her an expense paid family weekend at the theme park.

Tommy stopped spinning and stared at the skyline. "Wow, this is great. Look at all those rides." He'd worn the same baggy green shorts and sweaty shirt for the last two days.

Anna remembers deciding that he would shower and change clothes when they returned to the motel later in the evening, even though it would mean a fight.

========================

But there was no fight that night. And now more than thirty five years later, the slightly balding man who stands before her smiles awkwardly. "Mom? It's me, Tommy." His open-necked sports shirt has small sweat stains under each arm. "So you're living in Baltimore now." He called earlier in the week out of the blue. And that's exactly what he said, "I know I'm calling you out-of-the-blue, but finally - I tracked you down. You weren't easy to find."

She reluctantly agreed to meet him at a coffee shop on Charles Street not far from her apartment.

"It's good to see you, Mom." He gives her an awkward hug. "Luckily, I booked a flight into Baltimore for the weekend from Atlanta on short notice." Tommy glances toward the back of the coffee shop and says, "Let's sit at the booth in the back." He clears his throat. "You know on the plane I tried to remember the details of that summer when we went to Kings Dominion. You'd won some kind of free trip. Do you ever think about it?"

Anna slips into a seat in the booth. She'd dreaded this day for years. "No. I rarely think of that summer anymore." But she did think of that time often and just last week she was looking through a box of old papers and came across the small notebook she'd carried everywhere in her purse that year. She stared at the wish list that she'd begun and marveled at the careless slant of the handwriting of a person she had hoped to become.

Familiar guilt reminded her of a time when she added new wishes to the list almost daily: to live in Paris for a year, to speak French fluently, to dine in fine restaurants. She'd wished for a life that was glamorous, daring and unencumbered, any life other than the one she had. At the travel agency where she worked, she planned her clients' exotic trips as if they were her own, making certain her clients were comfortable with their dreams, while she herself engaged in daily fantasies. Perhaps some of her wishes, like a camera, might be possible. She'd begun to hide a small sum from her pay. Fortunately, Patrick never noticed that, or anything else she did.

Flying lessons were among the more daring items on that list. Her pulse quickened at imagining the nose of the plane lifting softly off the runway. Such freedom: to escape gravity's relentless pull. But when she discovered how expensive these lessons were, she set her sights on more modest possibilities, like photography or painting classes, as well as savoring less adventurous fantasies: reading in bed on lazy Sunday mornings, sipping fine tea, getting a silky Persian cat to hold in her lap. She had always wanted a cat, but Patrick did not like animals and Tommy had allergies. The realities of her life left a heaviness in her shoulders that made her feel forever earthbound.

========================

The waitress at the coffee shop brings Anna a cup of Earl Gray Tea and the coffee Tommy ordered.

"I'll never forget that day," Tommy says. "Someone drove us back to the motel. I remember calling Dad's sister, Aunt Betty and she drove all the way from Atlanta and got us the next day. She checked Dad into a veterans' rehab center and took me home to stay with her." He plays with a sugar packet before emptying it into his coffee. "You know for a long time I really hated you." He clears his throat. "You ruined that day for all of us. I remember how you got into a fight with Dad when he didn't want to ride around in a wheelchair and how mad you were when he did his old - *I've got a rock in my shoe* - joke."

Anna has forgotten that part. Once they were inside the park, Patrick refused to use a wheelchair. He refused to do anything with them that day. She took out her new camera to take a few pictures.

"You know I don't do wheelchairs," Patrick said. "And put the damn camera away." He limped to a nearby picnic table in the shade across from the restroom. "You all go on ahead on those rides," he said. "I'll set up camp here under this tree." He unfastened leather straps on his prosthesis with his good hand and tossed the plastic leg up on the picnic table with a loud thump. He removed the sneaker from the plastic foot and stared into the empty shoe. "Well, damned if I don't think I've gotten a rock in here," he said. He shook the shoe and laughed bitterly at curious stares from a young couple as they hurried away, averting their eyes from the stump. His right leg had been amputated just above the knee. It was a tired joke, but his favorite.

"That'll teach them to stare." He laughed and reached for his backpack.

"Please don't, Patrick. If they catch you drinking, they'll arrest you," Anna said. "You've seen the posted signs. Don't spoil this for us."

"Looks like they've got signs forbidding everything around here. Hey, you worry too much." He winked at her and nudged his cap over his red-rimmed eyes with his plastic hand. "No one really looks at someone like me. Makes them squirm."

========================

Now as she sits across the table from Tommy, Anna sips her tea and looks away. "Well, you threw a fit," Anna says. "Patrick had gotten you all excited talking about the amusement park. I'd brought my new camera hoping to get some nice pictures. But your father wouldn't ride anything. I didn't get many pictures before you ruined my camera. It's not a day I like to remember for so many reasons."

Tommy had kicked the picnic table at the park that day. "Let's go, Dad. You said you'd ride the Anaconda with me. I want to ride every roller coaster in this park." He turned at the sound of shrieks. "Oh shit. Look at how high that coaster is at the top. I want to do that one."

"They won't let me ride that stuff, Tommy." He pointed to a sign that listed rules for the various rides. "Of course, I can ride the carousel or the train that goes through the forest. Maybe that's what I need---a kiddie train ride. Toot. Toot." He shook his head. "I wish I had stayed at the motel so at least I could watch the Braves game."

"Damn it. Dad, you promised!" He threw his cap on the ground.

"Get over it, Tommy. It was all talk. I don't do rides anymore." Patrick shrugged. "Go. Just go. Ride whatever you want. I've got my radio. I'll listen to the game. Won't be the same, but when does anybody care what I want?"

"What?" he said in response to Anna's frown and groaned.

She tossed the camera back into the tote bag, and yanked it over her shoulder. "Come on, Tommy. What do you want to ride first?"

Anna followed Tommy to a line waiting for the Berserker, a ride that swung like a pendulum in a huge swooping circle, freezing upside down for a few seconds, leaving riders hanging upside down. How disorienting to hang like a bat. "Maybe you shouldn't do this," she said, but he raced to climb aboard when it stopped.

On the final swing of the Berserker, Tommy vomited.

When the ride was over, a tall, angry man confronted Tommy as he staggered away. "You barfed all over me and my kid." He put his hands on his hips. "You! I'm talking to you, boy! Don't you dare walk away when I'm talking to you!"

She pushed her way through the crowd as a park ranger intervened and handed paper towel packets to the man and to Tommy. "Happens all the time," he said. "You can clean up over there."

The man stomped away, dragging his young son.

"Did you see that guy's face?" Tommy hooted. "He was so pissed."

"Knock it off, " she said. "Do you want to take a time-out and sit with your Dad?" It was a threat that she had made too many times to be effective.

======================

Now years later facing each other in the coffee shop in Baltimore, Tommy says, "How could you leave me with that broken man? Then? Or ever! Do you have any idea how much he drank? "

"I'm sorry about your father, Tommy. He got a bad deal and made it worse for all of us. You weren't the only one injured." She leans toward him and says softly. "You know, after all I did to plan a fun adventure, it was a terrible weekend. You were angry and rude most of the time. And raising a teen-ager while strapped with a handicapped, alcoholic husband was no picnic for me either."

======================

Their first day at the park had gotten off to a rocky start, almost as bad as the previous day's tedious drive from South Carolina to Virginia. Traffic slowed to a nerve-wracking crawl on I-95 near the Virginia Welcome Center; the radio reported a ten-mile rolling backup caused by an overturned dump truck. Anna reduced speed in a line of cars that stretched for miles.

Tommy spent the last few miles making farting noises; now he began to kick the back of her seat. "Come on, Mom, drive faster. This is boring."

Anna wanted to say, *You know what! Sometimes I hate you.* But instead she said, "Tommy, stop doing that." How had he gotten so out-of-hand? Some of it was probably her fault. And living with Patrick's daily drunken self-pity made it worse. Most days she worked late. It was easier to let him watch television after dinner, but his grades suffered. She needed to do more; she wondered if other parents ever had moments of disliking their children.

She remembers braking sharply to avoid a car stopped ahead and Patrick mumbling, "What's all the shouting about?" He stretched. "Can't you two be quiet?" He fumbled with the clasp of his backpack. "God, I'm thirsty." He pulled out the bottle and took a quick sip.

He'd been sipping from a bottle of bourbon for the last few hours, and she couldn't prevent it anymore. For several years she'd taken him to AA meetings and she'd gone to Al-Anon herself, but he always found a store that delivered. While she was at work, he hid bottles all over the house. Once when she'd looked for a flashlight in the garage, she'd found more than a case of vodka hidden in boxes and bags in storage. He refused to let her have access to his veteran's checks, meager as they were. He spent all of it on vodka, and then when she decided not to fight it anymore, he switched to bourbon. He was intent on drinking himself to death. There was no hiding this reality from Tommy.

Anna pulled into a rest area. "I'm really tired of you both." She leaned her head against the steering wheel and took a few deep breaths; she reset the radio to a classical station, and returned to the Interstate. As their car crept past an exit ramp, Anna turned the radio off and pretended she was alone, her hands firmly clasping the controls of a small plane.

======================

The waitress returns with lunch menus and after she left, Tommy says, "I blamed you for all of it. But I know some of it was because Dad was so messed up from the war and the booze. He died a few months after you left. Aunt Betty became my guardian, but for a long time I thought you'd come back." He wipes his nose with his napkin. "Didn't you care what happened to me?"

"I knew that you were living with Betty. We were in contact a few times over the years. But after Patrick died, I thought you were better off with her. I felt I had done enough damage. I should have left Patrick. I should have taken you with me. I live with that. I've made peace with myself - finally - but it's taken more than thirty years."

"She probably saved my life," Tommy says. "She put me to work in her dry cleaning store in Atlanta and taught me the business. When she died last year, we had five stores; she left them to me, so I'm doing well. I'm married now and have a wife and two sweet daughters. And I've been wondering whether they should meet their grandmother. My wife Patty and I have talked about whether it's a good idea."

Tommy reaches into his pocket and brings out a small envelope of photographs. He hands Anna a photo. "That's my wife Patty, and my girls, Carly and Samantha." He thumbs through more photographs, selects three and pushes two toward her. "Remember how you trusted me with your new camera? And I took some pictures, and later I dropped it in the water on that ride?" The first is a picture of Patrick sitting at the picnic table, listening to his radio with his cap pulled low over his eyes. The second photo was taken at a slight angle looking up at the Anaconda with sunlight distorting the picture.

"You'd taken a few pictures, but I took some of these too." He patted the envelope.

"I thought that camera was ruined," Anna said.

"Aunt Betty took the film in for developing and some of those pictures turned out to be okay in spite of the water."

======================

That day at the park, Tommy rode roller coasters all morning and at mid-day Anna said, "We should go check on your dad."

"You go. I want to ride that coaster next." He pointed to the Rebel Yell.

"Can you wait here a few minutes?" Anna handed her new camera to Tommy. "Take some pictures. I'll be right back." She would risk it. "Then we can all have lunch together."

"But I want to ride the Ricochet and the Volcano Blaster. That's the one that takes you inside a volcano and shoots you out the top. I saw that one on television." He slipped the camera strap over his neck and took a couple of quick photos of her, the Anaconda and the Water Canyon behind her.

She was too exhausted to fight. "Okay. But please stay in this area and be careful with my camera."

When she arrived at the picnic table where they'd left Patrick, his backpack was on the table, along with two souvenir drink cups, but he was not there. She turned around to find him leaning on his cane behind her.

"Did you lose me?" he said. "I went to take a leak." He held a food bag under his arm. "Don't look like that. I've only had a few sips. I bought one of these souvenir cups for Tommy."

She put on her sunglasses. "Do you want to have lunch with us, you know, like a family? I left Tommy over near the cafe."

"Hell, no," he said, opening a bag of fries. "Don't worry. I'm all set. I've got my radio here. I'm listening to the game." He sat down, unwrapped a burger, and grinned. "Hey, I've got a funny story for you that I heard on the radio about a guy over in Georgia who was skydiving and lost his artificial leg. I mean, the guy's leg fell off and landed in a cornfield or backyard somewhere. Now picture this, he's on his crutches, hobbling around town handing out flyers that say, 'Can you give me a hand and help me find my leg?'" He laughed. "Get it?" He sipped his soda. "He didn't have a leg to stand on."

"Why do you think that's funny?" Anna sat down at the table and clenched her fists. "I wish . . ." Her voice trailed off. He looked so frail and pathetic to her.

"You wish?" Patrick said. "You wish! What **do** you wish? I mean, if you had three wishes, like in a fairy tale. What would you want?"

Anna thought about the list in her purse. She shook her head. "I don't know. It wouldn't matter what I wished for, would it?"

"Want to know what I'd wish for?" he said. "I bet you think I'd use one wish for my arm, one for my leg, and maybe the third one would be to not drink all the time, like I do now. But you'd be wrong."

He leaned over and looked at her closely. "I'd use one wish to cover it all. I'd wish I'd never gone to Vietnam. Without that war my life would be different, and I could still use my other two wishes."

"And I don't think we would have married," Anna said softly.

"Probably not," Patrick agreed. "But since you got pregnant just before I shipped out, what choice did I have but to marry you."

The war was winding down. President Nixon had promised to end it. Months later, Patrick returned with his terrible injuries. Now as she sat across from him at the picnic table, she took off her sunglasses and wiped her eyes with the back of her hand. His words stung, and while she suspected this unspoken truth between them, he had never said it before. She stood slowly. "Damn it. Stay here. Feel sorry for yourself, but I've got to go check on your son." She left without looking back.

As she walked across the park to check on Tommy, Anna was surprised to see a sign for the Eiffel Tower, a 275-foot-high platform that overlooked the entire park. Nobody else waited for the elevator to the top. She looked at her watch, hesitated, and stepped into the elevator. It wasn't Paris, but it was as close as she ever was likely to get.

The view from the tower provided a panorama of the amusement park and parking lots. Ant-like people waited in lines for rides. Food court roofs ringed the paved park walkways. People screamed amid the metallic clacking of the coasters. Off in the distance, I-95 highway signs and ramps routed traffic toward the park and motels, one of which was theirs where they would stay two more nights before driving home.

Anna wasn't sure what she'd expected at the top of the tower. Perhaps it was in that moment that her decision to leave took form. For she had hoped she might see a skyline, like the posters in her travel office. But off, beyond the highway, she saw abandoned cars sitting nose-to-nose, covered with matted vines in a junkyard. Vines that were, no doubt, crawling with restless insects living futile lives. Anna wondered how it would feel to be alone and free for longer than an elevator ride.

======================

The waitress returns to take their order for lunch. Tommy orders a BLT sandwich and iced tea, while Anna asks for another cup of tea. She has not been hungry since he called.

She looks across the booth at her son. He's grown into an attractive middle-aged man. He looks well cared for and his soft voice almost has a musical quality. Although she's been curious, she's surprised herself by agreeing to see him. He's almost fifty and she herself has recently retired from her job as an accountant in a law firm. She has missed so much. Avoiding pain has also meant avoiding joy.

"I tried to understand," Tommy says. "A couple of years ago, I started seeing a therapist. I have had so many questions. Betty refused to tell me anything, although before she died she told me to look in the Baltimore area. Where did you go that afternoon when you disappeared?"

"I drove," she said quietly. "All afternoon. Interstate 95 - until I had car trouble outside of Baltimore." Those days had taken on an unreal quality. "I stayed in a motel while the garage worked on the car; I became a tourist in the city." She needed money so she sold the car and found a tiny apartment downtown. "I got a job in a travel agency; I took night classes and got a better job as an accountant. I have mostly lived alone except for a couple of cats. Not a very exciting life, I'm afraid.

Although last year when I retired, I did take an Elder Singles tour of Paris."

"I have often wondered how you could be so unfeeling? Didn't you give any thought to what would happen to me and Dad?"

"Not at first. I was numb and actually considered suicide. So I have to ask the obvious question, Tommy. Why did you contact me now?" She wishes she had not agreed to this meeting. It brings up too much pain. She had an opportunity to see him again after Patrick died, but decided against it. She contacted Betty who angrily suggested she not return.

Tommy turns over the third photograph on the table and pushes it toward her. "This is the last picture I had of you." Tommy says. "This is why I had to find you."

Anna picks up the photo and catches her breath. "When did you take this one?"

======================

After lunch that day, she sat in the shade while Tommy went off to ride the Anaconda, a harrowing ride that dropped riders strapped into harnesses in an oddly restrained free fall, their flights stopping just short of earth.

She wondered how he could take pleasure in falling. It was not at all like her dreams of flight. In fact she'd had another flying dream the previous night. She dreamt she was flying over acres of cornfields covered with purple tassels. She'd flown close to the ground, with arms outstretched, naked, but comfortable, as damp corn tassels brushed against her skin. She'd felt an easy pleasure in the dream. And then, she touched the notebook in her purse and thought of Patrick's words and the hopelessness of her future.

A caricature artist sketched nearby. Anna stood up, stretched, and walked over to look at his work. He was sketching her face. He had captured her unhappiness, especially around her mouth, but what surprised her most was the sadness in her eyes. Because it was a caricature, the severity of her sorrow was even more pronounced, although her face was recognizable. After paying him five dollars, she studied the drawing and rubbed her eyes in disbelief. Then she hurried into the restroom, tore the paper to shreds, and flushed the evidence away.

She emerged from the restroom and found Tommy standing outside the restroom holding the camera.

"I took lots of pictures," he said. "I want to ride the White Water Canyon next."

======================

She'd forgotten that moment until now. Her hands tremble as she studies her younger self. She'd been younger than Tommy is now. What had she known about anything?

"You were sitting in the shade while I was in line for a ride and you looked like you were totally stoned or lost." Tommy leans over the table and looks at her intently. "Only years later, when I was an adult and realized what I was seeing, I couldn't hate you anymore."

======================

They argued because he insisted on taking the camera with him on the ride and tried to take pictures as he spun through the water tubes, but the strap broke and he dropped the camera in the water when he was getting off the ride. "Oops!" he said as he handed her the dripping thing.

Anna shook her head. She was furious. "Some vacation. Okay. Forget the stupid camera. I should have known you'd ruin it." She stuffed it in her bag. Maybe later she'd try to salvage it. The pictures taken earlier were most likely ruined.

"Sorry." He shrugged and wandered off to ride the Rebel Yell again. There he'd argued with another boy about which rides took the most guts to ride. Tommy called the boy an asshole and shoved him. Anna hurried over just as the boy's father appeared, red-faced and sweating.

"You shoved my kid." The man shook his fist in Tommy's face. "I'm going to have you thrown out of this park."

"I am so sorry about this." Anna grabbed Tommy's shoulder while he stared at the ground. "What were you thinking? Come on. Let's get out of here."

"Mom, I shoved that kid, but he was calling me names too."

They hurried back to Patrick, who was facedown with his head on the backpack at the picnic table. He had removed his artificial hand, which lay like a pink fish on the table. Burger wrappers littered the ground, and leaning over him, Anna smelled the stale bourbon on his breath.

She strapped on Patrick's leg and hand using quick, practiced motions and handed the ruined camera, backpack and cane to Tommy. Together they helped Patrick to his feet. He swayed and his cap fell off his head. Tommy picked it up and helped Patrick walk to a sheltered bench in front of the main gate.

"I'm going to get the car. I've had enough. Stay here."

Tommy held the bag with the camera and the souvenir cups. The stained backpack lay at his feet.

Anna walked to the parking lot. Sweat trickled down her back. She set the air conditioner to high and grasped the warm steering wheel, anger piled around her like dirty laundry. Years ago she had gone to the airport to pick up Patrick after he was first released from the VA hospital, and as he sat huddled in his wheelchair, she'd glimpsed her future and almost driven away from the airport without him.

She'd felt brave at the time, and afterwards decanted her supply of courage into tiny vials for daily use, but lately she'd begun to think more courage was required of those who left than those who stayed.

Now as she drove to the intersection for the parking area turnabout, she turned down the car's air conditioner and shivered. They were waiting to use up the rest of her life. She raised her eyes to a world beyond her car.

She tightened her grip on the steering wheel and took deep calming breaths. Patrick would remain slouched in an alcoholic stupor on a bench outside the main gate with his baseball cap pulled low over his eyes until someone noticed or Tommy thought to ask for help. She opened her hands. Red, feathered indentations marked where her fingernails had pressed into her palms. An entrance to the Interstate lay straight ahead. The sun was still high in the sky; there was plenty of daylight left. Plenty.

AFTER LIFE

Ted stood in the entry to the Egyptian mummy exhibition; his son's thin shoulder leaned into his hip and a wave of tenderness swept over him. He put his hand on Jake's head with its unruly sprigs of blond hair and marveled at his seven year old son's vulnerability. Perhaps Jake was too young for the exhibits at the natural history museum, but maybe he would like the mummy or dinosaur exhibits.

"Hey, buddy," Ted said, "let's go check out this new Egyptian mummy everyone's talking about." Their sneakers squeaked on the cool polished floors. The shriveled mummy lay in a glass-covered sarcophagus in the center of the Egyptian Room. Folded, blackened hands were clasped in a last grapple with death; its cheeks and skull tiny as a child's.

Jake pulled back, trembling. "This place smells weird." Dust floated in sunlight from narrow windows at the far end of the room. Cypress trees in the museum garden bent to a breeze, casting flickering patches of light on the walls.

Ted glanced over at his son as he moved closer to display cases along the wall. He bent to study a plaque. "It says here that this man was a famous stonemason who built beautiful tombs for a king. He lived in Egypt near a river and a desert." He put his fingers to his lips. "His museum's being renovated, so he's been loaned to this museum until the end of October, then he goes on to Atlanta."

"Dad?" Jake's whisper echoed off the marble floors and walls. "Can we go now?"

"In a minute. I want to read this stuff first."

"Dad, I saw a movie about zombies at my friend Andy's house. Aren't they kind of like mummies?" Jake touched Ted's sleeve. "I dreamed about something like that one time. Mom said I was having a nightmare when I told her about the zombies. But now I can't stay over at Andy's house."

Ted picked a small brochure beside the display. "So you can't stay at Andy's? Why not?"

"Mom won't let me. Can you talk to her?"

"Sure, Jake. Something like that happened to me when I was a kid." One summer Ted and his friend Jamie had camped out in the backyard while his mother was out of town. They awoke in the night to terrible screeching sounds and banged on the back door, but his father refused to open the door. "Don't be such wimps. It's just a screech owl," his father had said. "It's not like there was any real danger." He retold the story often, laughing at Ted's humiliation. But Jamie's mother never let him stay over again.

"I'll talk with your mother. Don't worry. Let's find out more about Egypt."

Ted opened the brochure. "This is interesting. Did you know that in Egypt they believed in the gods, Osiris and Ra, who helped the dead in their journey to the afterlife?" Ted smoothed his fingers over a plaque. "So they buried this guy with things he might need."

"Dad, are you sure this is not some kind of zombie? Could it lift up the top and grab people? Do you think he'll be mad that we're looking at him?"

"Nope. He's been dead a long time. His body is like an empty seashell."

"Where'd he go?" Jake asked. "Why is he a mummy?"

"I told you. He died and couldn't be a stonemason anymore." Ted put his arm around his son. "I'll bet you didn't know that I liked studying archeology in college. That's what this stuff is called. I wanted to be a hero like Indiana Jones and study ruins, but my Dad thought I'd be a better lawyer, so I went to law school."

"Who is Indiana Jones?"

"He was in these great adventure movies that I watched when I was a kid. Maybe I'll rent one for us to watch when you're over at my apartment next Saturday." It would be fun seeing those movies again with Jake. "Look! Over there is a chair and a bed, a case with his tools and weapons. They made mummies of his cats, dogs. Oh, and there's a hawk he probably used when he went hunting."

Jake hugged his arms to his chest. "You mean they killed his pets? Let's go, Dad. Please. Really. This is creepy. I don't like it."

Ted gently pressed Jake's shoulder. "It's okay. There's nothing to be afraid of here." He wished Jake were not so fearful. "Let's be brave."

Linda always gave in to Jake's fears. For a few months after the divorce, Jake had trouble sleeping. Sessions with a family therapist had helped, but Jake still slept with a light on when he stayed overnight at Ted's apartment.

Ted blamed Linda, who had her own odd fears. Often he had teased her about the way she hid in the bathroom during thunderstorms. She insisted it was a rational response to growing up in the heart of tornado alley in the Midwest.

Ted had talked with Linda last week about his concerns. "Jake is too timid. I'm afraid other kids will bully him."

"Well, Ted, you make it worse. Do you know how often you put pressure on him, on both of us? And he's just a little kid! Of course he's afraid." All of her anger of the past year gave way to pleading. "Why do you do this, Ted? Put so much pressure on everyone around you. All those long hours you worked, and still, you were the first attorney laid off when the economy tanked. You've got a chance to spend time with him. So why can't you help him, without making him feel so bad?" She had crossed her arms over her heart.

Now, standing beside the sarcophagus, Ted glimpsed himself in the reflection of the glass-walled case across from the mummy. Standing as he was with his jaw set, it was as if he were seeing his father's ghost. He willed his face to soften. "Jake, I thought you told me you'd like to see a mummy. But if you want to leave, we can go now. We don't have to do this. We'll go somewhere else. I saw signs for a couple of cool dinosaur exhibits over in another section."

Linda would probably call him later and rant that once again he had caused Jake to awaken with nightmares.

They left the dim room and walked through Native American artifact rooms. "Hey, those are real carved stone arrowheads. Indian tribes used them to hunt rabbits and small game."

Jake clung to his hand. "Dad, you know this morning when you picked me up, I thought you said we were going to see a Mommy. That's why I said okay before. I didn't know you meant dead people." His shoelace dragged, clicking on the floor. He tripped.

"Wait a minute, Jake. Let's tie that shoe so you don't fall." He waited for his son to tie the shoe, but Jake held his foot out to his father. "You tie it," he said. "Mommy always fixes it for me, because I take too long."

"Don't you know how to tie your own shoe? It's time you learned to do that." Ted bent down and tied the sneaker. "Look, I'll teach you how to do this when we get back to my apartment later this afternoon. Guys have to know how to tie their shoes."

Jake wiped his nose on the sleeve of his jacket. "Dad, I think people shouldn't kill rabbits." He sniffed. "I like rabbits. We have one at school. Sometimes I get to feed him. He makes a funny noise. He goes 'churrr-churrr' when I scratch his ears."

"Really. I didn't know rabbits made a noise like that," Ted said.

Jake wiped his nose on the back of his hand. "But, Dad, this one really does. He likes me. I feed him baby carrots."

Ted guided Jake to a nearby restroom. "Come on, Jake. Let's get some tissues so you can blow your nose."

On the way back to the main hall of the exhibits, Jake stayed close to Ted and ignored the other children who raced around chattering happily as they looked at artifacts from Native American regional tribes. Jake slowed to look at a large collection of feathered war bonnets and drums.

An exhibit featuring a replica of an encampment, complete with tents, campfires, and a spotted plastic dog, fascinated him. Plastic children frozen in action, chased hoops and waved sticks, stuck forever behind their glass walls.

Jake squatted and peered into the display. "Can we go in there and look at them?" He stood up and pressed both hands to the glass.

A security guard standing in the doorway called out. "Hey! Don't touch the glass. Sorry, but you can't do that." He leaned closer to Jake. "Don't touch." He glanced at Ted. "Sorry, but last month a kid ran into one of these cases. Cracked the glass and it hurt the kid, and it costs a bundle to replace that special glass." The guard softened when he saw the stricken look on Jake's face. "It's a museum, son. Look, but don't leave any marks. Okay?"

Before Ted could respond the guard turned and walked away.

"Dad, I want to go home. I don't like it here." Jake looked ready to cry.

"It's okay, Jake. You didn't do anything wrong." Ted put his hand on Jake's shoulder. "Come on, now. Don't cry. Be a big boy. We still haven't seen those cool dinosaurs yet. Mommy told me you liked dinosaurs. She told me Grandma gave you a book about them." He led Jake away from the security guard, who had stationed himself in a hallway outside the Native American exhibit.

They followed the signs to the dinosaur exhibit in the south wing and arrived just as a Cub Scout troop descended upon the exhibit. Scruffy boys in rumpled blue shirts and pants raced around the displays, stomping and calling out to each other. Their matching golden yellow kerchiefs were knotted around their necks, showing varying degrees of skill in assembling their uniforms. They dragged their hands over the glass-walled cases, leaving smudge marks.

The dinosaur exhibits held only a few small plastic replicas of early dinosaurs. "Well, that's not much of a dinosaur display," Ted said as they stood in the doorway of the exhibit. Most were about the size of a dog or pony. A plaque explained that the museum was conducting a fund-raising drive to build the collection. Although several exhibits were set up as archaeological excavation sites with plaques and layers of soil, Jake glanced at them with little interest.

Ted had hoped the dinosaurs would be larger, like the gigantic, fierce-toothed skeletons he'd seen as a kid when his parents took him to the Smithsonian Museum in Washington, D.C. His mother had taken a photograph of him sitting on the back of the massive fiberglass triceratops dinosaur replica at the museum entrance.

He remembered a book, *The Enormous Egg*, his mother had bought for him in the gift shop. Maybe that was the book his mother had given Jake. He made a mental note to ask her. He would look through her photo albums and find pictures of the trip to show Jake.

Jake scarcely looked at any of the displays. He followed along, scraping his sneakers on the floor, making high-pitched squeaks and marking the tiles "Dad, when can we go do something else? I'm hungry."

"Okay, let's go look around in the gift shop. Then we'll go get a burger."

The gift shop, a vast jumble of souvenirs, occupied a single ground-level floor in a central area of the museum. Multiple doors, each with checkout registers, opened into halls going to other sections of the museum, and glass walls looked out onto an open inner courtyard picnic area.

The Cub Scout group arrived in the gift shop, and noisy boys filled the aisles. A troop leader in ill-fitting shorts carrying a clipboard wandered around calling out names and checking them off.

Ted pulled out his wallet at the entrance of the gift shop and peeked inside. He had a couple of fives, a ten and a twenty. He was running low on cash, and he hated adding anything he didn't need to his credit card right now. "Okay, Jake, we need to save money for our burgers. And maybe we'll go to a movie later this afternoon. Find a toy or something that you'd like, then we'll go eat lunch."

Jake picked up a brown plastic *T.Rex* dinosaur. "Maybe one of these." He showed it to Ted. "Oh, wait." He picked up a heavy metal key ring with a blue palm tree museum emblem from a basket beside the door. "Maybe I should get this."

"Why do you want a key ring? You don't own a house." Ted laughed. "That's a special retractable one for car and house keys."

"It's for Mommy. She lost her keys. She's afraid somebody might find them and break into our house. She walked around last night locking the doors and she started crying. She put a chair against the back door."

Jake examined the key chain and the dinosaur closely. He held both out to Ted. "Okay, then I guess I'll take these."

"Well, the dinosaur costs four dollars and this key ring thing costs four fifty, plus tax. I think you should choose the one you want most. I'm running low on cash."

Jake's eyes were already filling. "But, Dad, can't I have them both?" He held the dinosaur and key ring up. "You said I could buy what I wanted. You did! You said it. And this is what I want." His voice had taken on a tearful urgency that Ted recognized as the precursor to a full-blown meltdown. "I really need these. I really do."

"I'm not giving you money to buy something for your mother, Jake. If you want the plastic dinosaur then buy it. It's a souvenir for you." He tossed the key ring back into the basket.

A woman waiting in line at a cash register turned and stared at them.

"But, Dad, you said I could choose." Jake took a key ring from the basket. "I really want this." He handed Ted the dinosaur. "I don't need this dinosaur as much as Mommy needs this."

Ted would have to let Jake buy them both. "So you want to spend ten dollars for this stuff! Oh, good grief!" How would Jake ever learn how to make wise choices?

The woman frowned and Ted lowered his voice. "Look, son, tomorrow I'll talk to your mommy about how to keep track of her keys. And I'll talk with her about letting you stay over at Andy's, too. Now here's ten dollars. Let's take the dinosaur and key ring to the cashier and pay for it. You need to learn how to do that."

At that moment, Linda called Ted's cell phone. "What?" he said. She always called at least three times on the Saturdays during his time with Jake.

He wondered if she did this because she didn't trust him or because she was lonely as he was on days when he couldn't see Jake. She said something about bringing Jake home early for . . . and then the spotty reception inside the sturdy walls of the museum cut him off.

"Jake, it's your mom. I lost the connection." He stepped out of the long line waiting for a cashier. "Stand here and hold our place in line while I call her back. I'm going to step into the courtyard to call her. I'll be over there. You can see me through the glass. Here's ten dollars or you can wait until I get back. I'll only be a minute."

"But I don't know how to do money stuff yet," Jake said.

"It's okay, son. You can do it. Wait here for me."

Linda called him back. She'd forgotten Jake was supposed to go to a birthday party at three. "It'll be good for him to go," she said. "He's almost never invited to any of the kids' parties. Can you get him cleaned up and drop him off by two thirty?"

Ted paced in the glass-enclosed courtyard. He had a stronger signal now, but he was tempted to hang up and turn off his phone. "I have a bad connection here, Linda." What would happen if he refused to bring Jake home early?

"Why do you do this when it's my Saturday?" He could see Jake through the glass wall between the gift shop and courtyard, still waiting in line, as he'd been told. Ted turned his back to the gift shop. He argued with Linda for a few minutes. He'd been late again with child support. She needed to get a grip, he told her. He was looking for a job. After all he was an attorney. He expected a call any day from a new firm that had interviewed him twice.

Finally he agreed to bring Jake home by two thirty, after they'd stopped for hamburgers. He lingered a moment, watching a family with two kids, about Jake's age, spread out a picnic at a table in the courtyard. It looked like a good idea for a Saturday afternoon. He was missing so much. It wasn't supposed to be like this. He'd hoped that he and Linda would have had a couple of kids. He wondered if he would have been better suited to raise a daughter, rather than a son.

Ted returned to the gift shop. But where the heck was Jake? He glanced up and down the aisles. "Have you seen a little boy with blond hair about this tall?" he asked the elderly woman cashier at the line where Jake had waited. "He was here in line only a few minutes ago."

"We've got lots of little boys here right now." The cashier waved her hand over a sea of Cub Scouts, many about the same size as Jake. "We've had three busloads in here this morning."

"He's not a Cub Scout. He's just an ordinary kid." Ted looked around the room hopefully. "Maybe he bought a key ring and a dinosaur?"

"I don't remember anyone buying a dinosaur and a key ring in the last hour," the cashier said.

"But he was in your line with a dozen other kids." He brushed his hand across his forehead. "I stepped into the courtyard to return a call and now I can't find him."

"Well, if he doesn't turn up soon, tell the security guard on this floor. I saw him going down that hall a few minutes ago. If you hurry, you can catch him."

"Well, Jake never goes far on his own. I'll check the restroom." It wasn't like Jake to play a joke. In the restroom across from the gift shop, Ted called, "Jake? Jake?"

Ted glanced under the stalls, but the men's room was empty. At first he'd been surprised. But now he was frightened. Why didn't Jake just do as he was told? He was supposed to stay in the gift shop.

Ted returned to the gift shop for another quick search with a growing sense of foreboding. It wasn't like Jake to wander off. He was much too timid. And why didn't he buy the dinosaur and key ring? The doors into the gift shop opened into other halls that looked alike. If he'd had left by one of the other doors, he could have gotten confused and be anywhere in the museum. Ted headed down the hall in search of the guard.

While he had lingered, watching the family in the courtyard, his son had disappeared. What if someone had grabbed Jake? Surely he would have called out for help. No! Most kids didn't realize they were in danger until too late and Jake was a kid who trusted adults. Ted couldn't stand to consider the terrible possibility that someone had taken his son. There was a simple explanation. All those doors had confused him. He'd probably gone out the wrong door and gotten turned around. Someone would help him. Most adults were kind and decent. Someone would find Jake crying, and soon Ted expected he would hear an announcement to meet his son somewhere in the museum. And yet, fear knotted in the pit of Ted's stomach.

Ted walked faster now, his knees unreliable. But what if something terrible had happened? He imagined his son's terror at finding himself kidnapped, or even if he was just lost, Ted remembered how he'd felt when he got lost when he was a kid.

He imagined Linda's frightened, angry voice. "What kind of father loses a child? Why weren't you watching him?" Linda would say, "How could you screw this up, Ted?" And she would be right. If he didn't find Jake soon he was a dead man. He wouldn't want to live if he'd let something happen to his son.

He had to find a security guard now. But what if they didn't find him? The question throbbed in his head.

Ted's wildest imaginings leapt ahead to a horrible scenario that he saw in a slow-motion montage: Within hours a citywide search for Jake would begin. Ted would face a police interview; he himself would be a suspect until they'd cleared him. But in the meantime, whoever had stolen Jake might escape with his son. Maybe the security team had captured what happened on surveillance cameras, or maybe not. Half the time those cameras weren't even filming. Maybe the family picnicking in the courtyard would not remember seeing Ted talking on his phone. Or maybe they would remember Ted on his cell phone, arguing with his ex-wife.

He had raised his voice at one point. He'd told Linda that she was "unreasonable" and the family in the courtyard had glanced at him. Linda had said, "Don't raise your voice to me, Ted." He'd been fighting with Linda, and all she'd wanted was to take Jake to a birthday party. She had called him a petty selfish man.

And it would get worse. If something unthinkable had happened to Jake, Ted had seen enough reality television to know that he would see Jake's face and name dragged across television, while Nancy Grace referred to Ted as "the worst dad in the world" or even "the person of interest in the Jake case."

He had an odd ringing in his ears. He had to find Jake. And find him quickly. He had read that the first few hours were critical in finding a missing child. He would retrace their steps. That was the rational thing to do. He shouldn't overreact. After all, he was an attorney. He always advised people to be rational.

The dinosaur exhibit was just ahead on the right. He went there first. It was the last place they'd been before the gift shop. A few Cub Scouts wandered around from the last bus, but most of them had already left. The early Saturday morning crowds had thinned out as people went off to have lunch on such a beautiful day.

Ted's pulse raced as he jogged through the halls and he tried to remember the order of the exhibits they had seen. As he turned down a hall toward the Native American regional tribes exhibit, he had a stitch in his side, as he often did when he ran without warming up. He passed the restroom where he'd taken Jake to blow his nose. He stopped to check, just in case. His stomach knotted with dread as he heard grunting sounds coming from one of the stalls. He pushed on the stall door. "Jake. Are you in there? Are you okay?" An old man, mumbling, came out of the stall with a newspaper tucked under his arm and hurried away without washing his hands.

Ted bent over and waves of nausea swept over him. He stopped and splashed a handful of water on his face, wiped off with a paper towel, and hurried to the next exhibit.

Even though the guard had frightened him, Jake had liked the artifacts from the Native American wing. And he might have gone back to look at the exhibit with the tents, campfires, and plastic children stuck behind their glass walls. Ted saw a boy about the size of Jake at the far end of the hall. He broke into a trot, and a sense of relief swept over him, until he got closer and saw that while the boy had a jacket like Jake's, this boy was with an older kid, and they were looking at arrowheads.

Ted hurried past two young women texting on their cell phones. He jostled an older couple walking slowly down the hall. "Sorry," he said. He stopped and caught his breath. "I've lost my son. He's about this tall and he's wearing a blue jacket and shirt, and brown pants. Have you seen him?"

"Oh no," the woman said. "I hope he's okay. I saw a security guard go that way." She pointed toward the Egyptian Room exhibit. "Maybe he'll help you."

The woman was right; it was time to ask for help. Ted jogged down the hall frantically hoping to find a guard. He didn't think Jake would go to back to see the mummy. He'd been too afraid, but at the entrance to the Egyptian exhibit, he bent over and rubbed the gripping pain in his side. When he straightened up, glare from the high narrow windows in the garden blinded him for a moment. At first he thought no one was in the room, until a small movement caught his eye and he saw his son.

Jake knelt beside the mummy's glass sarcophagus. A key ring with a blue palm tree lay on the floor beside him. Cypress trees in the garden cast shadows as Jake ran his hands along the sarcophagus, leaving marks along the sides. His words were a soft murmur that Ted longed to hear.

WAIT ON ME

I look up when this guy comes in and slams the door of my diner. Seems like he's pissed off, which strikes me as amazing on such a beautiful spring morning. He hesitates and I think he'll turn around and walk out, but the coffee seduces him. Truth is the coffee here enjoys an unearned reputation; it smells better than it tastes. Next thing I know he tosses his raincoat on a coat hook beside the men's restroom. That's how I know he's a pessimist. Today doesn't look like rain to me.

Well, this guy walks right past an empty seat at the counter and sits down at the booth. He takes up four spaces instead of sitting at the counter like the other loners. He's studying the menu like he's gonna be tested on it. He starts tapping his menu on the table. *Thunk, thunk* with the menu. Clears his throat and coughs, one of those fake cough that says, *Wait on me.*

I give Donna a quick nod and she strolls over to take his order. I pop an order of waffles off the griddle.

The guy thunks the table again with the menu and I take a good look at him. He's wearing a wrinkled tan and green striped sports coat. He has comb marks across sprigs of mousy brown hair, like someone dragged a rake across a dry lawn. He's the kind of guy people pity.

A couple of elderly women, Inez and Bea, from Sunnydale retirement village down the block, are here, just like they are every Wednesday; they give the guy a hard look and size him up like they do everybody.

This guy picks up his mug. "My cup's dirty," he says in a loud voice.

He nods to Donna and says, "Get me a clean one and make it quick."

Donna gets him a fresh table setting and frowns like she's found a bug on a salad plate. She's deliberate in her movements. She pours the guy some coffee and takes out her order pad.

I hear him say, "I'll have blueberry waffles."

Now all the regulars know me. I won't make blueberry waffles and don't have them on the menu. I won't mix fruit into batter. I have fruit-flavored syrups for people who crave fruit, but I'm a purist when it comes to waffles and pancakes. I've told Donna, and anyone else who'll listen, that I like honest food. I won't mix fruit into batter because fruit loses its identity. Donna's heard me talk about this for years. She says I'm weird.

So Donna tells this fella right quick, "Blueberry waffles aren't on the menu. Sorry." She glances over at me to see if I'm listening. "How about the buttermilk waffle special? Comes with coffee, a large juice and you can spoon blueberry preserves over it, if you like. And we have a great blueberry pie. I baked it myself."

I glance up and give her a wink.

"It's not the same," the man says. "So what's the problem with blueberry waffles? That's why I stopped here in the first place."

"Oh, try the buttermilk," Donna says. "They're really good." She gives me a look that says, *Why don't you just stir some damn blueberry jam into his waffles?*

The guy narrows his eyes and his voice takes on an edge. "Look here, if I wanted buttermilk waffles, I'd ask for them. You got some canned blueberries?" He holds the menu at arm's length and jabs it with a skinny finger. "All you do is take blueberries and stir 'em into batter. They don't have to be fresh berries. Why, it's so easy I'll bet you could do it."

Bea and Inez look over at the man and frown.

Donna rarely lets customers bother her. I know without even looking this guy's getting to her. She clicks the top of her pen back and forth. Lots of clicks. *Click. Click.*

I look up in time to see her put the order pad in her apron pocket as the guy starts in on her with, "What's the big deal? Come on. See what you can do." Then the guy reaches over, grabs her butt and says, "Come on. I'll make it worth your while."

I know trouble when I see it. I start to untie my apron and show the guy to the door when Donna decks him. She spins around and catches him across his face with an empty coffee mug.   Everybody stops talking.

Forks stall in midair, like one of those freeze-frames from a movie. The place is dead quiet until Inez, the old gal from Sunnydale, calls out, "Way to go, Donna!" Bea cackles. The two women clap and cheer.

The guy stands up and starts for Donna. She backs up to the counter, picks up a pot of decaf, and glares at him. He grabs his skinny jaw and spits blood into his napkin.

While he's distracted, I grab him by the back of his jacket and shove him out the door.

All I can think of is litigation. And I don't have time or money for some jerk's lawsuit. I'm barely making a living with this place as it is. So I step outside and say, "Hey, buddy, sorry about that. No hard feelings, I hope, but you got out of line in there with Donna."

He's wiping his lip on the back of his hand. "What a bitch!" he says. And for a quarter of a second, he sizes me up. I see the wheels in his tiny mind deciding against a fight.

A prudent move, since I'm still solid, after serving my twenty years in the Marines. Although I don't have time to work out now, I'm big enough that most men will back off.

I shake my head and try to help him see what's happened in there. "Things are different these days," I say. "Guys don't talk to women like that, and they sure don't go around touching them like that." I keep my voice even and I lean against the door.

He looks at me in disgust. "Damn women," he mutters. "Nothing but trouble."

I want to defuse this thing, so I shrug and say, "Donna's a good woman. She works hard and she been through a lot of bad stuff in her life. Cut her some slack. Lately she's been going to a women's self-defense class. Guess she needed to practice." I say this to ease the tension, but the guy glares at me.

He touches his split lip. He'll remember this morning every time he eats or drinks for a couple of days. I try to feel sorry for the guy, I really do, but he's an ass. I see how pale and shriveled up he looks out here in the morning sun. I feel good knowing I'm not gonna have to punch him.

The guy runs his hands down the front of his sport coat. "What's your name, fat boy?" He still has the napkin clutched in his hand. He clenches his fists, and his bony knuckles blanch white. "I'll have her job and yours too," he says. His voice shakes. "Who owns this dump?"

"Look," I say. "You're starting to irritate me. You can't come in here causing trouble." I put my hands on my belt and step closer to him. "I'm Jack. I own this diner and I'll stick by Donna." I stare him down. "Now get out of here before I call the police."

The guy throws the napkin on the ground at my feet. He crawls into an old blue Taurus and drives away, leaving a cloud of exhaust fumes floating over the parking lot.

I figure that's the end of it. I go inside to smooth Donna's ruffled feathers. Don't know how I'd run this place without her. She's a bundle of energy and everybody likes her. I hired her the first week I opened the diner two years ago.

She's on her way back from the restroom. She storms around muttering under her breath, and her eyes are red.

I need to tend to my grill, but I hate to see her so upset. Not many people know this, but I've found myself attracted to Donna. Truth is I've never really had a girlfriend, but I drove past her house on my way to Mass some Sundays and wondered what she'd say if I asked her out. I finally got enough courage to ask her to dinner a few months ago.

I felt like a teenager. I guess it was more of a crush, although I'm a little old for that, but for the first time in my life I got weak in the knees at the smell of her shampoo. But it didn't work out. I've never had good luck with women in the long term. Maybe I wait too long to let them know how I feel. Guess that's left a strain on our working together.

I still have some breakfast orders waiting. But Donna won't let it go.

"Who does he think he is?" She rages around wiping tables with a red striped towel. The towel makes an angry flapping noise.

Alvin, one of my regulars, who owns the Amoco station down the street, perches like a crow at the counter. "Whoa," he says. "That was harsh! Somebody woke up on the wrong side of the bed today."

Donna puts her hands on her hips and glares at him. She's got the towel in a death grip. She whirls around to face me like I'm the one who offended her.

Alvin shrugs and pays for his breakfast. "Don't think the guy deserved that! You'll be lucky if he doesn't sue you."

I shake my head to warn Alvin to give it a rest as he heads to the door. I hear Donna behind me.

She slams a saltshaker down on the countertop. "I don't need to let some sleazy shoe salesman put his hands on me." She's breathing hard as she says this.

I lean back against the counter. I'm never sure how to deal with angry women. I don't know what to say. That's probably one reason I stayed single all these years. It's just easier to avoid all that drama. I wait for her to calm down.

The two women from Sunnydale pay their check and leave Donna an extra two-dollar tip. "Don't worry, honey. It'll be okay," Inez says. "Good riddance to him, I say."

The other regulars gulp their coffee and leave money for their food on the counter. They slide out the door, leaving a couple of uneasy customers who still need their breakfast orders. They're sitting at the counter pretending to read the paper.

I hurry to get the rest of the food plated and served. Donna's standing so close I can smell her shampoo. "Salesman," I say quietly. "How do you know he's a salesman?"

"The creep left his raincoat," Donna says. "I went through the pockets and found these." She yanks the coat off the hook, reaches into a pocket, and pulls out a packet of business cards. She shakes the coat at arm's length, as if holding a dead thing. A plastic credit card falls out of a pocket. Donna turns her back to me, steps on the card, and in a few minutes she picks up the card, and slips it into her pocket.

I realize she doesn't know I see what she's done.

"He's a salesman for Jarvis Shoes over in Belton." She waves the business cards fastened with a thick rubber band. "His name is Roy Price."

"Let's forget it," I say. "Guys like that cut and run when someone calls them out." The remaining customers are standing up to leave. I pick up money from their tables.

"Maybe I'll teach him a lesson and throw his raincoat in the Dumpster out back." She starts toward the back door.

"Don't do it, Donna," I say.

The last breakfast regular, a senior citizen who never wears his hearing aids, counts out the exact change for his tab on his placemat, folds his newspaper, and shuffles out. We're alone and probably will be for a while. Time enough to get set up for the lunch crowd before they start to file in a little after eleven.

I take a couple of deep breaths to give Donna a minute to think about what's happened. I flip up the *Closed* sign on the front door that says *Lunch 11:30–2:00*.

Now I don't believe in revenge. Maybe you take a poke at someone if they really get out of line and that's the only way they'll get it, but I like having whatever's going down settled up front. No grudges.

"Come on, Donna," I say, "let it go." I ring up the tickets and count the money in the register. I hope the guy doesn't sue us. I don't think I have enough insurance to cover a lawsuit. I feel bad. Maybe I should have done more. I realize nothing's settled here.

I feel foolish, like I did when I finally got the courage to ask Donna out. I took her to a nice restaurant for Sunday night dinner. I thought we'd had a good time and it was great to have somebody else cook for a change, since I never open the diner on Sundays. I'm still not sure what happened between us. But when I made my move, she looked surprised. She said that I wasn't her type. She was sweet about it, but she said I was a friend; she needed more, if she was going to take a chance on anyone again. I didn't know what to say, so I joked that I didn't mean what she thought I did. I told her I was not interested in a serious relationship at my age. My lie still gives me pain.

Donna wouldn't even look me in the eye for weeks after that. I guess I gave her mixed messages, but I was afraid she was going to quit. I've waited, trying to get up enough nerve to ask her to reconsider. We were beginning to get things back on an even keel, and now this happens. I've never understood what causes women to flare up like that. I'm surprised by her outburst. She's not given to anger. That's one of the things I like about her, although I realize now that I don't know her as well as I thought I did.

She tosses the guy's raincoat back on the hook. She flicks the towel over her shoulder and stands with her hands on her hips. "Look at me, Jack," she says.
I hear the quiver in her voice. Maybe this is about something more than that guy being an ass. I stop ringing up tickets and look at her. Her mouth is soft and turns up at the corners even when she's not smiling. It occurs to me she dyes her hair. Her eyes are puffy from crying.
Her voice catches as she says, "I've been pushed around most of my life." Her eyes fill. "I never intended to

cause you trouble." She sits down at the counter and covers her face.

"What is it with men?" She says this softly. She turns around and looks at me with a fierce expression. "My dad used to beat my mother. My ex-husband was a bully, too. I don't want to keep making the same mistakes all my life." She wipes her eyes with a towel. "I want someone who's not afraid to be honest enough to admit a mistake and make it better."

I stand behind her. Trying to decide if I should go over and put my hand on her shoulder. Be a natural response, I think. But she seems too injured, like a bird that's crashed into a glass window. I'm afraid to touch her. But I'm glad, even now, that I didn't touch her at that moment.

I don't know what to do. I open the stainless steel cooler. A cold mist rolls out of the refrigerator. I let the cool air clear my head. "Let's get those lunch specials ready," I say. "So are you're still going to that women's center for those self-defense workshops?" I glance over at the clock.

"I'm learning to take care of myself." She slips the credit card out of her pocket. She thinks I don't see her do it, but I catch a glimpse out the corner of my eye.

"Guess I should call that guy." I say. "Tell him his raincoat's here." I stack up tomatoes and lettuce from the cooler. I glance up at the Pepsi clock over the grill. "The lunch special today is a BLT or a tuna melt. How about writing the specials on the chalkboard for me? Oh, and could you get me one of the guy's cards? I'll call him so he'll know he's left his raincoat."

"I threw his cards in the trash," Donna says.

I go over to the trash can and fish out one of his cards. I speak to Price's boss and say he forgot his raincoat at my diner, but she says she doesn't expect she'll ever see him again. Says she fired him. I decide not to mention it to Donna. She's finally calmed down.

The day slips by in a rush after the lunch crowd swings in for salads, soup, and sandwiches.

About three o'clock, I'm cleaning the grill and putting together a supply order list, but I'm curious about what Donna plans to do with the guy's credit card. I see her at the old pay phone in the hall by the restrooms. She's been at that phone a couple of times today. Then I get it. She's using the guy's card to charge stuff. Maybe phone sex or horoscope readings. She gives the guy's card number and lays the phone down, leaving the meter running. That's cold. I should have told her the guy lost his job.

Someone will probably trace those calls. Almost nobody uses a pay phone anymore, except the down and desperate. I make a mental note to have that phone removed. I need to hang it up. I need to say something to her about revenge and the trouble it brings.

She's grinding coffee beans, but before I can say anything, Price walks into the diner.

"I came to get my coat," he says. He stalks to the back and pulls the coat off the hook. "Figure you owe me a cup of coffee to go," he says. "Black." He nods his head slightly. He touches the little cut on his lip.

"Okay," I say, thinking maybe he's about to apologize to Donna. I still don't feel sorry for him, even if he has lost his job.

"I'll get it," she says. She turns around and pours a large cup of steaming coffee into an insulated cup. She pops on a top and hands the coffee to me. "No charge. It's on me. Let's just forget it."

Price sneers. "Last time I'll stop in this dump. Even my ex-wife could make waffles!" He takes the coffee, flings the raincoat over his shoulder, and slams the door on his way out.

I had hoped she would apologize to him, but now I've changed my mind. Maybe she should have put salt in his coffee. "What a pathetic ass!" I glance over at the phone.

I want to say something about forgiveness and how hard it is to ask for it. I want to tell her all men aren't bums. Instead, I say, "I'm sorry. I probably should have made the guy happy and fixed his waffles. Then you wouldn't have had to deal with him."

She looks surprised. "Maybe. But then you wouldn't be the stubborn guy we've grown to love, would you?" She smiles for the first time all day.

I keep thinking about saying something about revenge and how no good ever comes of it. Instead, I just stand there like a fool, with my hands in my pockets and I let the phone stay off the hook a little longer. Waiting for the right words.

RABBITS

Early in the eighties when we had the chance to buy land and build a house in upper state South Carolina, we grabbed it, although my wife, Alice, who was particularly close to her family, dreaded the thought of leaving Charleston. "It's only four hours away," I reminded her, "not too far to drive down for a weekend. This was after the incident happened to our daughter, Mary Ann. A crazy boy in her eighth-grade art class went on a rampage. He slashed out with sharp pointed scissors—a random act, they said—and cut a gash across the side of her cheek while she sat drawing a charcoal sketch of a pony. The wound healed leaving only a faint scar, but that was the moment when I realized the world was going mad and I needed to get my five kids to some quiet safe place, away from violence.

Perhaps it was the missing connections to nature that caused people, crazed by noise and traffic, to be unpredictably violent, even in a sleepy southern city like Charleston.

After the builder finished the house and barn in January, I went with the movers a week ahead to get the house organized while Alice and the kids stayed with her mother. The builder had gone bankrupt before he'd finished the landscaping around the porch and deck; the meadow behind the house was rough and muddy in the gray light of a winter afternoon. I made plans to plant trees and shrubs by spring. But finally we had a house large enough for our family, built the way we wanted it, just as I had promised Alice when we married.

My four daughters had mixed reactions to the move. Cindy and Mary Ann, our oldest daughters were angry about leaving their friends. And our two younger daughters, Joan and Lisa didn't want to leave their grandmother, but they all calmed down when I agreed to buy a pony.

I located a farmer who sold us a young gelding pony and a calf; he even sent over a flock of chickens in a crate. Our youngest boy, Clint, barely three years old, was intrigued and terrified by the chickens. While I was building a fenced yard for them, he would kneel and make cautious clucking sounds at the crated fowl, cringing when they lunged pecking and squawking at the bars of the cage. The kids were amazed to discover that if they looked in the straw-filled boxes in the chicken yard, they would find brown, smooth eggs that they could hold to their cheeks to feel the warmth. Joan and Lisa would follow me out to feed the chickens carrying colorful baskets to gather the eggs. For a while they didn't want us to cook them, in case there were baby chicks inside them, so I had to buy our eggs at the store.

I gave the youngest kids a brief explanation of the life cycle of chickens using a fair amount of creativity, knowing that they'd get more details later when Alice felt that they were old enough. She had sturdy opinions about waiting until they asked more complex questions. She'd waited until the two older girls were each twelve before she'd talked with them about sex.

I admit I was relieved to be let off the hook, but I worried that some day my youngest girls would wonder if I was dishonest or just stupid.

After Clint was born, we knew that five kids would be our limit. I wouldn't have minded another boy, but Alice was clear that this was it. So we focused our attention on raising happy kids in a safe rural setting.

I hurried home from my job teaching high school math every day and set about planting cherry, apple, plum, and dogwood trees. Alice was homesick, and no matter what I did, she seemed depressed. I feared that she would decide to take the kids and move back to Charleston. So I planted two pecan trees in the front yard to help her deal with her distress at living in the "sticks." Alice's mother had three ancient pecan trees in her back garden on Wentworth Street that Alice loved.

By May, after school was out, I felt we'd turned a corner in our new life. Most days we settled into a calm routine and were glad for it. I'd grown up on a farm and hated farm chores, so I joined the Marines for adventure, until I met Alice and settled down. Now I discovered that I loved planting a garden and landscaping the yards. I even arranged to have a guy with a bulldozer come over and build a small pond so the kids could fish and play with frogs, as I had as a kid.

Alice and I loved hearing the excitement in the kids' voices with every new discovery. Each day felt a bit like Christmas to me.

Early that summer our middle daughter, Joan, the busy third grader who often thought up mischief, had asked at breakfast if she could buy two rabbits. "I'll use my allowance to feed them," she said. "I can buy two with the money I got for my birthday."

"No," Alice said. "No rabbits." She had answered before we could talk, although we exchanged looks. The kids saw this and sensed a divided front. I knew not to undercut her decisions, but sometimes after we talked privately about something, she'd change her mind or I would change mine. "We're overrun around here with animals. I don't want to be the one having to take care of them. So no."

We didn't know then that Joan had already bought a couple of rabbits from a neighbor's son. Little did we know, even as we were discussing it, the rabbits were huddled in a pen in an old shed behind the garden!

I didn't particularly mind the idea of rabbits, although I remembered from grade school that it didn't take long for a couple of rabbits to multiply in a way that brought new meaning to the term *geometric progression*. But I trusted Alice's instincts about what our kids needed.

We found out we had rabbits the next day after this discussion. Lisa, our first grader, had gone outside to feed the new pony a slice of apple, and she ran into the kitchen while we were having breakfast. "We have lots and lots of rabbits." She was jumping up and down. "Come see. Baby bunnies. Everywhere. Tons of them."

The whole family almost trampled me as they raced to the backyard to count ten baby rabbits.

Alice groaned at the wiggling mass of babies and looked at me.

"I didn't know," I said. "Honest. I never told Joan yes."

Joan said, "Davy sold me a boy rabbit and a girl rabbit. Please let us keep them." She brought one of the tiny babies to Alice, who stroked its tiny pink face, while the kids marveled that its eyes were sealed shut. "They're blind? Why are they blind? Will they be okay?"

I told her lots of animal babies can't see at first, so their parents protect them from danger while they are helpless. And then, as I examined the other rabbit, I said, "Well, good news! You don't have a pair. But unfortunately, the other female is going to have babies soon, too."

Alice shook her head and sighed. "Oh, good grief! Okay, I give up, but you all have to help and your father will need to get to work building more pens. When they get old enough, you'll have to find homes for them."

So we let the kids keep the rabbits. How could we say no? I spent the next Saturday afternoon building sturdy hutches with fine wire mesh and runs behind the old tool shed. I added a wire fence and a gate that the kids could open and close by themselves.

A week later the other rabbit gave birth to twelve babies. And a month later, the girls talked me into letting them care for a friend's rabbit while they were away. But Thumper chewed through a wall into a pen that had the first female in it, and after that things got a little out of hand. By August we had at least thirty rabbits. Although we gave some away, I soon lost count of exactly how many we had.

The kids named them all, and it was quite a sight to see the girls walking around in the backyard followed by a dozen rabbits. They taught some to hop along beside them on a leash. Another one would chase a ball. They played with those bunnies like they were puppies.

But one morning in early August, I looked out the window and saw a pack of dogs circling the chicken yard. I raced out and chased them away. I learned from a neighbor that a family had moved away and left their dogs to roam the neighborhood. Other dogs had joined this ragtag pack. I worried that they might attack the girls and cautioned them to throw rocks at them to scare them away. I considered buying a gun but decided against it with so many kids around.

Later in August, Alice had been especially quiet at dinner one night, and after the kids were safely tucked into bed, she told me she was worried that she might be pregnant again. "You promised me this wouldn't happen! I don't have the energy for another child," she said. "I really didn't want a half-dozen children and I told you that when we married."

I was both happy and sad for us. But what could we do? I vowed to find a way to do more to help. Maybe I could tutor students and get some extra money. Maybe we could get someone to come in and help with the kids. Maybe one of her sisters could come from Charleston for a while when the new baby came. We would find a way.

And I admit that although I adored my beautiful girls, I did hope the new baby would be a boy so Clint could grow up and be someone's big brother.

In September for the long Labor Day weekend we arranged for one of our neighbors to feed the animals. We piled into the station wagon and drove south to Charleston to see Alice's family. It was our first trip back since we'd moved. Alice had arranged to see her doctor, who'd confirmed the pregnancy. She was sad and resigned, but we'd decided we would make the best of the situation.

We decided to wait a while before telling the kids about the new baby. We had a good visit, and just before we left to drive home, Alice told her sisters and her mother, who reacted with surprise and sympathy. As I packed the car for our drive home, I really feared that Alice would change her mind and stay in Charleston. So I was relieved when she finally said her good-byes and got into the car.

She cried quietly for a while as we drove home. The kids kept asking me what was wrong. I told them she missed her mommy and sisters. The kids were quiet and I could tell it worried them to see Alice cry like that.

At one point when we stopped at a rest stop, I came back to the car to find them all crying. "We all want to go back to Charleston to live," Joan said. "We don't need rabbits and chickens. Why did you have to make us move?" That four-hour drive seemed to last for days.

Clint was asleep when we got home just before time for dinner. I carried him inside to finish his nap and started to unpack the station wagon. The two older girls went off to see a new friend who lived nearby. The two younger girls, bursting with pent-up energy, leapt out of the car and raced off to see all the animals.

A few minutes later I heard terrible screams, the kind that every parent fears. A scream that tells you something horrible has happened. A scream different from any other sounds you'll ever hear, and even now, remembering it, the hair stands up on the back of my neck. I dropped the suitcase I was carrying into the house and met Alice running down the stairs ahead of me. "Oh my God. What's happened?"

When Alice and I got to the backyard, both girls were crying hysterically outside the fenced rabbit pens. The torn wire gate lay on the ground beside the cages. Hutches were ripped open; many were upside down with the doors missing and the wire mesh torn and scattered.

Joan held a back leg. Lisa had an ear. Both were screaming and their hands were covered with blood. For a moment, I feared they'd been attacked by whatever had brought such carnage.

I took a step and something crunched beneath my shoe. A white paw. I stood in a killing field and around all those overturned rabbit pens the ground was covered with the remains of rabbits. Tufts of fur blanketed the grass. Tiny puffs of it floated in the air.

Alice knelt and gave me a look of reproach. She held both girls while I walked around the area, trying to make sense of what I was seeing, but how could I make sense of the horrible work of a pack of stray dogs that had been allowed to run loose around the community all summer? Clearly it had happened just before we'd gotten home. Some of the bodies were still warm.

The girls broke away from Alice and we ran from cage to cage, lifting the wrecked doors and looking into the backs of hutches for survivors. They found two. One young doe was so badly injured that she died the moment I lifted her from the ruined cage. Her soft black-and-white fur stuck to blood on my hands. The other rabbit, a small white one that Lisa had trained to chase a ball, lay on her side in shock, until I gently slipped my hands under her to examine her.

The minute I lifted her, she emitted a high-pitched tortured sound that made me dizzy with fear. The girls were pleading with me to take her to a veterinarian, but that was impossible. The nearest vet was a half-hour drive. As I felt the damage to her underside and warm fluids trickled from her nose and mouth, I knew what I had to do.

I looked back at Alice and said, "Honey, take them to the house and get a shovel." I wanted to cover my ears to stop the awful sound of that poor rabbit, but instead, I slipped my thumb just behind the base of her head along her spine. I whispered, "I'm sorry, I didn't mean for it to be this way," as I pressed as mercifully as I could. She twitched once and went limp in my hands. I felt her heart thrumming a few more feathery strokes through the fur on her chest. Her eyes glazed over and she was quiet. I had never killed anything, not on the farm or as a Marine, and I hope never to again.

My shoulders shook as I stood holding that rabbit; I'm not ashamed to say I cried.

Alice and the girls returned with a shovel. They watched as I set about digging a hole. Then Alice helped the girls gather rabbit remains into their egg baskets.

They brought them to me. We buried the rabbits and the baskets near that oak tree at the far end of the garden. The carnage of a pack of wild dogs on a beautiful fall afternoon is hard to explain to children. I put my arms around Alice and the girls as the sun was going down. The sky was red behind the shed that housed our chickens, left untouched, but addled, by the violent rampage. And I knew there was no safe place.

KINDNESS

Evan drove his aunt Louise to the dump along the back roads of rural South Carolina on a hot July day. Home from NYU for the summer, Evan had yielded to his mother's pleas to spend a few days with his elderly aunt Louise. "She called and asked if you would visit for a few days to help her clean out that firetrap of a basement. I've been after her for years to get rid of that clutter. She won't let me near her stuff, but she trusts you not to throw out anything she truly loves."

Louise's ancient Buick labored under a full load of cast-off household junk.

"Just listen. Let her talk," his mother had said. "I know she goes on sometimes, but it's hard to be alone." In her old age, Louise took pleasure in following the local gossip, passing along even stale news to others. Evan thought of her fondly, though. Lately he'd considered whether he should finally tell her that he was gay, but he feared the news would be hard for her to understand. He had not even told his parents yet.

He had spent many summer days at her house. He'd had a happier childhood because of her kindness.

They'd spent the better part of the last five days sorting through boxes of unfinished sewing projects, books on gardening, out-of-date clothing, and ten-year-old magazines, before tackling broken lamps, clocks, toasters, radios, and remote controls, but in the end, Evan persuaded her to sort out three piles: things to keep, to give away, and to discard at the local dump. Evan had driven usable items to the local Goodwill center. He'd spent the morning packing items beyond repair into plastic bags and loading them into the car so that only one trip to the dump was necessary.

"Don't forget to tell me in plenty of time before we turn off the highway," Evan said, interrupting his aunt's steady monologue about her garden club's show. In spite of Evan's fondness for his aunt, five days of her nonstop talking had grown tedious. The sluggish car pulled toward the shoulder of the road, and he wondered when she'd last checked the tire pressure. While he was uncomfortable driving her aging Buick, the thought of Louise driving unnerved him. Her eyesight was failing.

As they passed a small country church set off in a stand of pines, Louise grabbed Evan's arm. He swerved on the winding road, startled. The car slid in loose gravel on the shoulder of the highway. A large rock struck the underside. "You scared me, Aunt Louise."

"Oh dear, sorry, but that cemetery reminded me," Louise said. "Did you hear about that young boy they found murdered in a cemetery near here last fall?"

"You know I don't get local news when I'm away at school," he said, his voice sounding sharper than he'd intended. He didn't want to hurt her feelings. The old woman had taken to pouting silences when she believed people were being rude to her.

"I'm sorry," Louise said. "I didn't mean to grab your arm and frighten you. I just wanted to tell you about the murder. The *Gazette* had a story about the family. In fact, I seem to remember that the boy's uncle worked at the new dump. And the boy had worked there part time." Louise shifted slightly and looked at Evan. "Are you sure you never heard anything? Why, that murder was all over the news," she said. "A couple on a picnic found him a few miles up the road from here. Only seventeen and laid out on top of a gravestone like a sacrifice. It hurts my heart to think of it." She sighed. "They interviewed his mama on TV and it was the saddest thing."

Evan nodded. He'd seen something about it on the Internet, and although he had not known the boy who was killed, the story made him uneasy. The Internet story had suggested the boy was gay. But the local gossips would most likely only whisper that the boy was gay. He imagined the local news coverage would focus on the tragedy of a prank by bullies that went too far.

He himself had seen a bit of it. He'd been bullied throughout high school, but now that he was away at NYU he saw a different world, one somewhat removed from these pressures. What could anyone say about a story like that? "Someone just killed him for no reason. That's horrible," he murmured. His aunt focused too much on the misfortune of others. She'd never done that when he was younger.

"They showed his picture and he was so handsome." Louise said softly, "He looked like that actor from the *Titanic*, that movie you rented for us a couple of summers ago. Such a lovely young man! Not much younger than you. And every bit as handsome." She stared out the window. "What's that actor's name?"

"Leonardo DiCaprio?" And although he didn't really want to know the gruesome details, he found himself filled with both dread and a hopeful curiosity that the killers had been caught. "Did they arrest whoever killed him?" Evan asked.

"Oh no. I'm sure they'll never find out," Louise said. "Seems like he was a gentle boy. Wouldn't hurt a fly." She leaned toward Evan and whispered. "They said he was one of those pretty, poetry kind of boys. That's what we called young men like him in my day."

Evan knew what his aunt was suggesting. He wondered why people of his aunt's generation were so hesitant to say aloud a simple word like *gay*.

She turned and looked at Evan. "In spite of his good looks, he didn't like girls, if you know what I mean." She leaned closer and whispered, "I wonder if that's why they killed him? That's what they said at my garden club."

He glanced over at his aunt, who sat rubbing her lip thoughtfully.

"I saw something on *Oprah* about it," she said. "I have learned a lot from watching television. But I still don't understand mean people. Why can't people just let people be?"

Evan could not imagine how much enlightenment could be gleaned from television, but he was touched by the idea of his aunt's efforts to try to understand.

"Give me some warning before we turn off the highway," he reminded her. "I've never been over to this new dump." A new clunking noise came from the front end of the car. Evan cocked his head and listened. He worried that he had damaged the car when he'd swerved on the rough gravel shoulder and run over that large rock. His mother would be annoyed if he'd done any damage.

"Don't you worry, I will." Louise didn't seem to notice the noise. She straightened her cotton print dress and sighed. "Preacher Gray preached a whole sermon about that boy at church. He said that a debt was owed and paid. He said we needed to remember that 'the wages of sin is death.'"

"Are." Evan said. "The word *wages* is plural. '*The wages of sin* are *death*.'"

"Not in my Bible," the old woman said. "That's what's wrong with the world, you know. All the changes in what's said and not said." She folded her hands in her lap piously. "The preacher said the unjust are denied the good Lord's mercy."

"Oh, Aunt Louise, surely you don't believe that," Evan said. "Not about that poor boy. You know, that's part of the stupidity that makes me so angry about how the South still treats people who are different in this day and age. That preacher doesn't know about kindness or love. He's a jerk!"

"Now, watch your mouth, Evan," she said. "I hope they didn't teach you to be an unbeliever up in New York at that college you go to." She turned to look at him. "I think the preacher is wrong." She seemed about to say more, but stopped herself.

"I just hate bigots," Evan said. "That's why I can't bear to live here in the South anymore." Surprised by his outburst, he felt as if he'd broken some unspoken rule between them.

"Oh, don't be so grumpy." Louise moved closer and patted his shoulder. "So good to have you spend time with me," she said. "Why it seems like yesterday you used to visit me every summer. You were just a tiny boy, and now here you are driving my car." She laughed. "You were always into mischief. Remember that time you threw all my fresh ironing into the bathtub and filled it with water? I couldn't get mad. You thought you were helping me with the laundry. You were always trying to help."

Louise chuckled. "And remember that time when you were about nine? You put on my old shoes and a dress that was so long it dragged on the floor. And you pretended to teach the first grade, just like I did. You had that old cat of mine sitting in a chair. You told me you thought you could teach him to read."

"You were such a sweet, funny little boy. I always felt like, if I'd ever married and had a son, he'd have been like you." She fell silent for a moment. "Well, I'm too old now to teach the first grade or keep track of a cat. But I do miss it all." She paused. "And you, I've missed you."

"I remember," Evan said, softly. His aunt's face had wrinkled, leaving her skin dusty and transparent. She didn't have many more years. He glanced over at her. "Remember how we'd go over to Leider's for ice cream on Saturday afternoons? Big double-dip cones with chocolate and pecans?"

She reached over and put her hand on his shoulder.

As they drove up a steep hill, the engine on the old Buick groaned. Louise cupped her hand behind her ear. "Evan, this car is making a funny noise." She gazed out the window. "You know, I just keep thinking about that murder. They said he had car trouble, too." She looked thoughtful, as if she were sifting her memory, looking for lumps. "On TV, his mama said he was such a sweet boy. When he got killed, he was on his way home from driving his ragtag car to get pills for his grandfather." She leaned forward and rapped hard on the windshield. "That's the place. Right up there."

Evan slowed, thinking his aunt meant to show him the road to the dump. Instead, she pointed to a white brick church beside the road. "Found him over in that graveyard beside that oak tree. They did terrible things to him." She clutched at Evan's arm with cool hands.

Evan didn't want to hear more. She was on the brink of telling dreadful details. "Sorry to interrupt you, but I seem to remember a sign along here for the dump."

"Why yes, but we have to call it a landfill nowadays. The paper says the county plans to plant trees and make a lovely park out here once they fill it up. All that trash will be covered over." She suddenly slapped her hand on the seat. "That's the road."

The car strained as Evan braked at the county's green-and-white landfill sign.

Louise switched off the air conditioner. "Try that," she said. "Maybe that'll help." She opened her window a crack and chuckled. "Now this place is called a recycle center. Everything and everybody is recycled," she said, "and it kills me the county supervisors act like they invented the whole idea. They promised this landfill would never smell bad." She rolled her window all the way down. "We're close."

"Yuck. Roll it up," Evan said. "I'd rather be hot." He drove the car past an iron gate onto a dirt road thick with ruts. Up ahead a red bulldozer had cut large open pits through acres of fields. "Now what?"

"Well, I guess you should back the car over next to that hole," Louise said. "I think that's what you do." She turned around in her seat to watch. "Careful, Evan, don't run over that man who's walking up behind you."

The man stood beside the pit waving, "Come on back. Closer. Ease it on a little more. That's good."

Evan hopped out, opened the trunk and the back door of the Buick. He pulled a couple of plastic bags onto the ground. "We've got a ton of junk," he said as the man ambled over to the car. "I'm helping my aunt clean out her basement."

Louise got out of the car and walked around to stare into the open pit. "Look at all the wonderful things people throw away." She pointed to a cracked wooden chest and a faded plastic flower funeral basket. "Now don't you just know somebody could use that?" She closed her eyes when Evan threw a broken kitchen chair and toaster over into the hole. "Hate to see them go," she said. The air was heavy with moist clay and decay.

Evan tried not to breathe deeply as he piled bags, broken lamps, and debris near the edge of the pit. It was filled with garbage and household junk. He'd never seen so many ordinary objects reduced to their essential elements. Televisions lay in the midst of stoves and tattered clothing, reminding him of CNN tornado scenes.

"Wait and let me help you with those bags," the man said. His curly gray hair crept from under a smudged red Atlanta Braves baseball cap. His blue watery eyes looked like he'd been too long in the sun without sunglasses. Hitching up his overalls, he smiled a toothy hello and limped around to help. "I'm the manager of this establishment. I'm also the hired help, the backhoe operator, and sometimes the dozer driver. I do it all." He laughed at his own joke. "My family used to farm this land, but after we sold it to the county they hired me to keep it going."

"Well, it's kind of you to help us," Louise said. "My nephew here is home from college and I put him to work cleaning out my basement. "She stood, hands on her frail hips, and supervised while Evan and the old man emptied the trunk. "You stay out here in this heat all day long?" She fanned the air. "Must be hard to take on a summer day." She rummaged around in her pocketbook. Finding a white lace handkerchief, she shook out the neat, ironed folds and held it close to her nose. "Mercy." She waved the handkerchief at the old man and laughed. The scent of lavender from her handkerchief called up Evan's memories of childhood summers following the old lady around in her herb garden.

The man shrugged as Evan slammed the trunk. "It's not bad," he said, "better than farming, though it's mighty warm today." He mopped his forehead with the back of his hand and tossed bags in a practiced sweeping arc to the deep open pit below. The bags burst open with a shushing sound. "You sure packed a lot into that car."

"They ought to give you extra pay in the summertime," Louise said, wiping her face. "Do you live out here in that old shed?" She motioned to a rough frame building at the edge of the woods. "It's good that the county gives you a job and a place to stay."

The old man looked surprised. "Oh, no. I don't live here." He pointed to the wooden shed. "That's my office. I keep a few comforts there. Got a TV for slow days, running water, coffeepot, but no phone. County won't pay for a phone." A red truck was parked under a tree behind the shed. "And I'm not about to get one of those silly pocket phones."

"I guess you can get used to anything," Louise said. "At least you can stay out of the heat." She shook her handkerchief toward the old man as Evan maneuvered her into the car. "Well, we'll be on our way."

"Thanks," Evan slammed the heavy car door. His aunt seemed oblivious to the patronizing effect of her words on the old man.

She sat calmly wiping her face. "Oh, I meant to ask him about his nephew that got killed," Louise said as she settled into the Buick's big front seat.

Evan hurried to start the ignition before his aunt embarrassed him any more. The engine sputtered and stalled. Smoke boiled out from under the hood. He muttered under his breath.

"Oh my," Louise said. "It's never done that before. Now our goose is cooked. Why, it must be a good eight miles into town. We'll have to ask that man to help us."

The man ambled over to the car and motioned for Evan to release the hood latch. He raised the hood and poked the wires knowingly. Lowering the hood gently, he wiped his hands on a rag from his pocket. "Better let a mechanic work on this," he said.

Evan got out to look.

"Know much about cars, son? I didn't think so. You college types never learn how to fix things that are broken. But, I have to say, I thought maybe a wire was loose, but I can't fix this." He pointed to oil pooling under the car.

"Oh dear," Louise said, opening the window. "Stranded at the dump."

The man walked around the car and leaned over next to the passenger-side window. "I'll drive you into town." He took off his cap. "The Exxon mechanic can tow your car in and fix her up, I'd guess. Give me a minute to wash up and I'll drive you to town in my truck."

While they waited, Evan kicked himself for forgetting his cell phone. If only he'd driven his Honda instead of his aunt's clunky Buick, even if he'd had to drive two trips.

At that moment the man drove up in his ancient truck, that was waxed to the sheen of a fresh candy apple. He tooted the horn. "Climb in." He reached across the seat and opened the door. "My name's Easter. Easter Clarke."

Evan helped his aunt get settled into the seat beside the old man. Then he squeezed in beside her. "Thank you," she said. "You've saved our lives, Mr. Clarke. She looked around and ran her hand over the rolled leather seat. "I'm Louise Abelard and this is my youngest nephew, Evan. I don't know what would have become of us if you weren't out here looking after things at the dump," she said breathlessly. She surveyed the road from her perch. "Goodness gracious, this truck sure is high off the ground." She clutched her pocketbook close to her gaunt chest. "Well, now, Mr. Clarke, you have an unusual name. Easter, is it? Why, I don't suppose you're going to say you were born on an Easter Sunday."

"Yes. Yes, I was," he said. "I suppose that's kind of an unusual name, though."

That's lovely," Louise said. "It's a novel name, Easter Clarke. I mean, sounds like a character in a book is what I mean." She smiled nervously, the wrinkled corners of her mouth tilted up.

As they bounced along the dirt road, Evan studied his reflection in the side mirror. He needed a haircut. He tucked a strand of hair behind his ear. He would arrange to have the car towed. And he hoped he would not need to stay too much longer to help his aunt deal with this problem. He'd planned to drive to Charlotte on the weekend to see his new boyfriend, Rick, before he left for Italy.

Easter swung past the gate at the landfill and turned onto the highway.

"I was thinking about the terrible murder over at that churchyard that's down the road from here," Louise said. "I was telling my nephew, Evan, about it this morning. He's been away at college in New York and hadn't heard about it until now." She tested the waters carefully. "I understand the boy was your nephew?"

Evan wished he had thought to caution his aunt not to talk about the crime. He imagined the kinds of questions she was likely to ask. Details she was sure to share later with her church group. Private things not covered on the local news. She was relentless when she explored a topic.

Easter Clarke changed gears and the truck picked up speed. He rubbed the gray stubble on his chin. "Well, Miss Abelard"—he compressed his lips as if making a decision—"Kenny was my sister Lucille's youngest boy and it's just about killed her." He swallowed hard. "Truth is, we're pretty tore up about losing Kenny."

"Oh my goodness!" Louise said, "How terrible! I saw his picture on the news. And that must've been your sister I saw on the news. Such a handsome young man! He looked like that movie star from the movie, *The Titanic*. It shakes my faith to see how terrible the world has become."

"Well," Mr. Clarke said after a long pause, "I don't think the world is terrible; just some mighty terrible people live in the world. But it sure shook my faith." He tightened his hands around the steering wheel. "Shook my faith in God, I'm sorry to say." He wiped his nose with the back of his hand. "Not a day goes by we don't miss Kenny."

Easter looked ready to cry or lash out somehow.

Evan pressed his elbow gently against his aunt's bony side, hoping to signal her to let it alone.

Louise glanced at Evan out of the corner of her eye. She pulled at a string on her handkerchief. "Do they have any suspects? I mean—do they know if he was killed by someone he knew, or maybe somebody killed him because . . ." Her voice trailed off.

Evan tried to think of some appropriate distraction so Louise would shut up.

The veins stood taut on Easter Clarke's neck. He said, "Well, since the sheriff didn't arrest nobody yet, I guess we all pretty much figure some local boys killed him. We hear rumors, but no one's talking." He glanced at Louise. "Local boys. Isn't that what you'd figure?" Rage seeped from his voice. "Thugs who got nothing better to do."

"It's so sad," she murmured. "I don't know how his poor mother can bear it. Why, I saw a talk show just last week about what murder does to families."

Easter Clarke gripped the steering wheel; the bones of his hands shone white under his skin. "I'm the one the sheriff asked to look at the body to see if it was him. No one deserves to die that way." He wiped his face on his sleeve. "I live haunted by it."

"How terrible." Louise's hands fluttered to her mouth. "I'm so sorry, Mr. Clarke, I shouldn't be prying into your pain. I can imagine how hard that was."

Evan glanced at his aunt and realized he was slightly pleased by her discomfort. She was both repelled and fascinated, like people who sat riveted while talk show hosts exposed private tragedies in ways that disconnected from the reality of genuine pain.

"I don't think you *do* know anything about it, really! That boy went through hell." Easter's anger swept over them and his breath seemed to catch in his throat. The truck sped along the highway, going faster by the minute. "Imagine what you would have felt," he said in a voice too loud for the limited space of the truck. "They tortured him." He swung his right hand into a fist and struck the wheel.

But the old woman seemed to shrink beside him now. Her fragile blue-veined hands folded like shriveled bats in her lap. She bit her lip.

Evan was sorry for her. As the horror of what had happened to the boy swept over him, he could not imagine the magnitude of such loss. He was sorry for them all.

The truck swerved onto the shoulder of the road, bounced along the rough asphalt seams, and careened back onto the highway. Evan glanced at the speedometer. They were well over the speed limit.

Louise grabbed Evan's hand and squeezed it hard, her fingernails curled into the base of his thumb. She trembled beside him. "Oh, my," she murmured. She turned to look at Evan with watery eyes. "Oh dear me."

Evan fought back the panic rising in his throat. "Please, Mr. Clarke," Evan said. "Slow down. You're scaring us." He wondered if he could find a way to signal a passing car for help. "Mr. Clarke, please slow down."

Easter Clarke's voice dropped to a whisper. "Kenny must have hoped, even prayed, that someone would help him." His chest heaved and he sighed.

The old man eased his foot off the accelerator and he glanced at the two passengers as if seeing them for the first time. "I am sorry," he said, "for all of us, living in a world like this."

Grief was everywhere in that truck.

Evan's eyes stung with the sudden weight of it.

For a moment Louise sat still and stiff beside Evan. Slowly she eased her grip on his thumb. Her hands were dry, like brittle leaves against his skin. Color rose in the old woman's cheeks.

"Easter," she said, gently touching his arm, "I have no words that'll bring comfort to you. There is no comfort for such a loss." The air was fragile. "We are so easily broken by the meanness in the world and the pain it causes."

The old man stared straight ahead and blinked. Finally he said, "I'm sorry that I unloaded all those hard feelings on you. I had no call to do that." After that, he said nothing for the few remaining miles.

"I don't know what happened to me back there," he said as they pulled up to the gas station in town. "I'm ashamed. I've never done anything like that before in my life." He drove them around to the front door of the Dixie Exxon.

Louise put her hand over the old man's hand, which rested on the steering wheel. She did not speak. He started to say something, then his eyes filled and he looked away as Evan helped Louise out of the pickup.

Easter waited with his engine idling, watching until he was sure someone would help them. Evan waved to him from behind the smoky glass window of the station after he spoke with the mechanic, who agreed to drive them home and tow the car. Easter nodded and drove slowly out of the parking lot.

Evan imagined the old man's lonely drive back to the landfill with his emotions scattered like spent rifle shells all around him in that truck.

Louise was strangely subdued. When the Exxon mechanic dropped them off at her house, she went upstairs to her bedroom and lay down for the rest of the afternoon.

While Louise rested, Evan opened the door to the basement and sat on the stairs. Now in the soft light, he saw a clean well-ordered storage space. The house seemed lighter now because of his efforts. He had helped.

He would ask his mother to take Louise shopping for a pretty dress to wear to his graduation at NYU in December.

She'd never been to New York. Last night he had told her about the graduation. And also that in January he would move to Chicago to work as an editorial assistant for a magazine. The thought had a bitter sweetness that surprised him.

She'd been happy for him, but he sensed her disappointment.

He looked up when he heard the gentle scuffing sound of Louise's slippers on the stairs. The sound made him ache for what had been and what was lost.

Evan prepared a light supper of rice, butter beans, corn, and sliced tomatoes from the garden and iced tea for his aunt. Louise sat at the table and examined a brown age spot on the back of her hand. "I used to have beautiful hands," she said as she studied the bent fragile bones in her fingers. "I always meant to learn to play the piano."

"Where does the time go?" She looked up at him and her eyes were round and moist. "Evan, honey, I feel so old. There is so much I meant to say and do, but didn't."

Evan swallowed hard. Tomorrow afternoon he would drive her over to Leider's and get double-dip ice cream cones, like in the old days.

"Supper's ready. I fixed your favorites," Evan said, heaping his aunt's plate with rice and beans. "I was worried about you. I was about to come upstairs to see if you were okay."

Louise poured herself a glass of iced tea and patted Evan's arm. "I've been thinking about that poor boy and his uncle all afternoon. What must it be like to be caught up in such meanness? To be needing the kindness and understanding of others?"

She wiped her faded blue eyes with her napkin. "Evan, I keep thinking that we've never talked about it. But maybe we should. That could have been you." She sipped her tea and shook the ice gently in the glass.

UNNATURAL DISASTERS

I worry about world peace, corrupt politicians, breast cancer, and why water collects in the bottom of my refrigerator. I worry that the odd tingling sensation in my left breast is cancer, or maybe it's just the beginning of an early menopause. I worry about what has happened to my cleaning lady, Brenda.

Last week I noticed that Brenda, failed to place the hairbrush in my bathroom in the regular spot by the sink. This is the second week in a row. I worry she is getting sloppy. She is taking me for granted after five years. Or maybe something's going on with her.

The only worry I can deal with today is the refrigerator, so I stay home from work and wait for the repairman. I worry he won't come. While I wait, I read in *Reader's Digest* that people who worry are rehearsing mentally for life's worst-case scenarios. Disaster films play in their heads. The article says worriers spend energy in futile attempts to be prepared. I'm reading this article because my computer network is not working this morning. I'm prepared to wait until after lunch before calling the help line. Sometimes my computer heals itself. I'm prepared to wait.

Be prepared. I think of the Scouts' motto. I was a Girl Scout and I remember I worried, even then, about being prepared. Just in case, we were told. Always carry money for a phone call on a date. That was before cell phones changed that. I wonder what kinds of advice girls get now in the Girl Scouts. I think there is some kind of link between worrying and scouting. Maybe compulsive young women become Scouts, or perhaps the experience, during a formative period, welds us to our prepared state.

Worry, the article in the magazine says, wastes human energy. If that's the case, I waste a lot of energy. I never feel prepared enough. I am not prepared for many of life's nasty little surprises, in spite of my best efforts and good intentions.

Take breast cancer. I read the statistics and know the probabilities. I watch my friends discover breast lumps and they are never prepared. I'm not prepared. Never will be. I'm scared shitless. I'm in the highest risk group: women over forty who never had a child or breast-fed one. I wonder why these two things are listed separately. Seems to me one must occur before the other—a prerequisite. I should have prepared. Should have lowered my chances decades ago.

I think of calling my doctor and scheduling a mammogram. I worry they will find the lump I'm not prepared for. Perhaps I've waited too long to prepare, let alone have a mammogram.

Now as I look around the house, I realize that someone else is cleaning. The kitchen towels are folded wrong. Brenda is precise. A stickler for perfection. And predictable. Someone else has dusted and left books piled haphazardly on tables.

While I wait for the refrigerator repairman, I check the phone number twice to be sure it's right and I call the agency to ask about Brenda.

"Just a moment," the secretary says in a thin voice. "I'll need to let you discuss this with someone in management." She pauses a moment and says, "Can I have someone call you back in a few minutes? Will you be at this number?"

I get a cloth and dust the living room while I wait. I straighten the books and notice that the windows need to be washed on the inside. I write a reminder to Brenda.

She has a key and lets herself in on Wednesdays. On Tuesday nights, I always worry that I will forget and set the deadbolt. I forget sometimes and have to drive over from work to let her into the house. I rarely see her. The agency hired her, sends her, and takes care of the paperwork. I use an agency because I once considered running for city council. I worried that some improper paper trail might seal my fate, but now, I have changed my mind about running for political office.

There are too many social issues beyond repair. I am prepared for something I've decided not to do.

Brenda and I send each other notes about things that worry me, like the spot where the cat throws up under the table in the living room. I scrubbed the spot and watched the stain grow larger. It left the carpet discolored. I wrote Brenda a note. *Needs something stronger*, I say. Later, after Brenda removes the stain, I worry that the chemicals she used are dangerous. I worry about her and the cat.

All stain gone, she wrote on the bottom of my note. *Next time leave spot alone. You make stain worse. Old cat! Die soon?*

Once when I spent a Wednesday in bed with a cold, Brenda brought me a cup of soothing honey-herbal tea and we talked. Of her early years in Haiti, of her grown daughters and her dream to retire to Florida. I told her I was divorced and recovering from years of treading water in a tedious relationship. Told her I regretted not having children. Wished I had daughters.

She sighed. "I remember my old mother used to say, a woman yearns to take back the best of her past, but must live in the present." She adjusted the shade in my bedroom window so I could see the autumn leaves falling from the maple trees, and she smiled. "We can only anticipate a little," she said. "Everything else is luck."

Brenda is much older than I am. She reminds me of my mother's older sister. She is small and precise in her movements, with a voice that flows like ribbons waving in an island breeze.

After we talked, I always pictured her brown eyes in my mind as I wrote her notes. I cannot bear to ask her to do any more really awful tasks. I think of my own mother and I am thankful she is not cleaning someone's house.

I think about Brenda and I worry. Why hasn't she left me a note for the past two weeks? Has she retired and moved to Florida to live with her daughter? At least, I think, she'd say good-bye. I worry I've offended her somehow.

The manager for the cleaning agency calls me back. "Brenda," the manager says, and she clears her throat a couple of times, "is no longer with us. Is the new person, Reba, unsatisfactory?"

"Reba?" I say. "Who is that? Where's Brenda?"

"We can send out someone else, if you like"

"What do you mean, Brenda is no longer with you? Did she retire?" My voice is too shrill. "Don't tell me she quit?"

The manager hesitates a moment. "This is quite difficult," she says. "Awkward, to say the least. I had planned to send a note."

"I hope you didn't fire her," I say, worried the agency has treated Brenda badly. "She does wonderful work."

"Brenda is deceased."

I sit in silence. Unprepared. "How?" I whisper. I'm thinking heart attack and regret the times I asked her to clean behind the sofa. I look at the note beside the phone. The note that I've just written, asking her to clean the windows.

"Unfortunately, she was killed. Stabbed by her boyfriend. Two weeks ago. It happened right after the holiday. All the local news channels covered the story."

I realize I do not know Brenda's last name. Five years she helped me and I don't even remember her full name. I probably saw the news report and thought it was just another stabbing.

"Oh no." I feel my throat closing up and I cough. I can't think of anything useful or appropriate to say. I mouth the word *boyfriend*, but for Brenda, the word *boyfriend* doesn't sound quite right. I can't imagine this.

The manager takes my silence as a cue to say more. "We all loved Brenda," she says. "We saw the bruises and worried about her. We told her to kick him out."

"Did they arrest him?" I ask, and I worry he could still be out there. Perhaps he's got keys to all the houses Brenda cleaned. Maybe he'll break in to steal. And kill again. The thought repels me, because I think it at a time like this, and because I know he could be out there, waiting, and I'm not prepared.

"He's dead, too. Killed himself when the police came."

She says this and I feel relieved. I notice that I need more compassion and an alarm system. My eyes burn as if I'm standing downwind from a fire.

"So tragic." She says this and I hear her blow her nose. "It happened on a Tuesday night. We almost canceled, but Reba agreed to add you to her list."

I thank her for telling me and hang up the phone. I don't want to know any more. I go into the bathroom and pick up my hairbrush. I look at the yellow bristles for a long time. I notice more gray hair in the hairbrush than usual. I stare at my aging face in the mirror and think of disasters. I know we're never really ready.

Someone knocks at the door. And I wonder, as I put my eye to the peephole, if the man I see is really the refrigerator repairman.

THIS ARROW MARKS ME

"Lose the breast?" My lips go numb with disbelief. As if I could lose my breast and suffer only the mild regret of leaving my breast, like my favorite pen, at the bank. I am in Dr. X's office, getting good news and bad news, but right now I don't know which words are intended to be good news. Words like *mastectomy*, *malignancy*, and *metastasized* wash over me. Words surging, in and out of my head, like ocean tides. I imagine myself rowing frantically against stormy seas. Salty spray runs down my face. The word *recovery*, repeated, has an odd echo effect that leaves me dizzy.

An overhead speaker softly plays a song I once liked, connecting it forever with this moment. I watch Dr. X's lips moving, out of sync with his words, as he shows me x-rays. He will refer me to a female surgeon, as I have requested.

He says that Dr. Y is a fine surgeon. She specializes in a range of reconstructive procedures to make the whole experience less traumatic. I listen to his hollow good cheer and wonder how often he gives this wretched news each day. I imagine he does not let himself know what women feel when they're told they will lose part, or all, of themselves. He's unlikely to lose parts of his body. I wonder if he has a wife or daughter.

As if reading my thoughts, he reaches out and touches my shoulder lightly. "Helen, may I call you Helen? If my wife needed this surgery, I would want Dr. Y to do it." He tells me his office will contact Dr. Y's office with test results and set up a consult as soon as possible. "The trick," he says, "is to live, to defy this terrible disease."

I leave his office and walk with unreliable knees past the receptionist as the office background music shifts abruptly to tinsel-type tunes played like carnival music, an artifact used in amusement park carousels, but here it is played softly to drown out reality. I recognize strains of a tune from my childhood and I remember as if I am ten again. I am longing for a pony, but the bay on the carousel in the park is the only one I ever get to ride.

I had gotten the phone call a week ago to come in to discuss my recent mammogram. My heart thumped wildly as I lowered myself into a chair and wrapped my sweaty hands around the phone. As if I'd never feared this moment. "Yes. I could come in to see the doctor and schedule more tests on Friday. I will need to cancel meetings."

I have so much to do right now. I'm much too busy for this. I think of the stack of unfinished book reviews I am editing for the magazine where I work. And who will do my department's quarterly reports due in two weeks?

I hang up the phone, having agreed to additional tests, a course of action sure to alter my life. I know this even as I run my hands over my offending breast. I feel betrayed by a close friend. Stung.

I regret my lifetime of uncharitable complaints about my body, harsh words used to describe my breasts as I stared at myself in clothing store dressing room mirrors.

Perhaps now I will pay the price with my pound of flesh. I am tempted to ask my body for forgiveness, but I hardly know where to begin. I resurrect a prayer from childhood and chant it like a mantra against the inevitable, a tuneless song of hope.

I arrive early at Dr. Y's office. I fill out insurance forms and my hands smudge the ink. I agree to pay whatever my insurance won't cover. Spare no expense. As if I could refuse to pay the hospital after losing my breast. But what if I did not have the insurance that permits Dr. Y and her team to cut, stitch, and restore me?

I regret that I never got around to taking out a disability policy and must dip into my savings until I can work again. I wonder if I should call my ex-husband about all this, but I remember how busy he is now with his new wife and children.

Perhaps I should have confided in someone at work, but I hesitate to share my troubles at work. I tell my co-workers that I am taking a few days off to deal with a personal matter. Maybe I should call my sister in California.

I return the forms to the receptionist and settle into a hungry leather chair to wait.

I scan magazines on the tables. Stacked neatly next to *Time* magazines are specialty magazines with headlines touting clothing geared for women with special needs and marketing prosthetic devices and underwear for those of us whom surgery has rendered hard to fit. Some magazines show sexy underwear, promising that passion is possible post-surgery.

Of late, I have considered the idea of passion rarely. Until now. But before the bad times in my failed marriage, I once lived on tender slices of joy rendered by a touch. I have taken my pleasures too lightly. Gazing now into what appears to me to be a cataclysm, I hope that the best of what has been before, will be again. I vow to live.

Here in the waiting room, almost everyone whispers. Quiet murmurs blend with soft background music and the solicitous flutter of soft voices, then footsteps, as a nurse leads one of the women waiting with me into a hallway to an examining room. As they walk through the doorway, light from the hallway forms a shimmering aura of soft pink and purple around them, as if their bodies ride waves of fear and hope.

Compassion is mixed with custom, but these nurses are subdued, for they know how little separates us at this moment. It's a matter of dots on a screen, an unwelcome density. For we know we are women, all of us, likely to be spirited away through time's portal for a test of our endurance.

A slender young woman in faded jeans, leather jacket, purple socks, and Birkenstock sandals checks in with the receptionist. "Oh, Olive," the receptionist says. "You look wonderful." A nurse in her early thirties comes out to greet the young woman and they hug. Olive slips out of her jacket and slings it over her shoulder with careless ease. She smiles and her short curly hair looks like new growth on a hillside after a forest fire. Her eyes burn defiantly. She wears a purple shirt with the words *Proud to Be* in large white letters across the front, and on the back of her shirt are the words *Of the Clan of One-Breasted Women*. The lines are credited to a writer, Terry Tempest Williams. Olive wears no bra and no prosthesis. Her shirt lies flat against her left chest; her shoulder slopes forward slightly, as if resisting a weight. I think of the empty sleeve of a war veteran.

Our eyes connect and she smiles. She is like a particle at the point of open awareness, as if a magnifying glass has focused light and heat through her. Energy from her body touches me and I am warmed.

I look down at my breast, lying quietly under my blouse. I try to imagine my body without the weight, the warmth of blood, the substance of tissue, but I cannot. I wish for an elixir, a potion stronger than anything produced by medical arts.

The nurse puts her hand on Olive's right shoulder and leads her to a nearby examining room. They stand outlined for a moment in the soft light. The door to the hallway and room is ajar, slightly, for only a moment, but long enough for me to overhear the nurse say, "So you've finished the chemo and the tests look great. That's good news."

The nurse returns and nods to a frail young woman who is probably in her early twenties, calls her Betty, but she looks too young to be a patient. Surely her breasts are still prepubescent buds. She sits alone in a corner near a fake potted palm tree, as though relishing shade at an oasis. Her body seems transparent, faded by the struggles of the flesh. Her fragile features and baldness remind me of a doll, Miss Fritters, from my childhood, who lost her hair as a result of an accidental overnight soak in the bathtub.

As the nurse leads Betty away, she turns to me. "Helen, you're next," she says.

Ceiling music swirls above my head. The smell of my fear is thick, sweet, and leathery, like pony sweat on a summer afternoon. I am ten again and filled with fear for my first pony ride. I soothe my fear tenderly until I am calm enough to stand and follow the nurse into the hallway. I ask for a glass of water and the nurse leads me to a water fountain. She hands me a paper cup that I must hold with both hands. I sip but cannot swallow. I glance at the swaying floor as the nurse's sturdy white clogs move toward me. She guides me to Dr. Y's office. My brain feels unavailable, as if it's left the office. I am surprised to be so frightened still.

Dr. Y greets me in her office, her face sincere and concerned as she shakes my hand. She shows me pictures of varying shades of gray. The invading white masses are circled and she points to charts with my breast outlined in red Magic Marker. She speaks softly of possibilities and probabilities. She gives me hope, as she talks about survival rates, but she includes the grim realities as she hands me pamphlets that explain what I've just heard and forgotten. I had written questions to ask Dr. Y, questions that shrivel in the back of my throat, while my notes lie curled and forgotten at the bottom of my purse. My arms are clasped to my sides. I try desperately to keep my body from bursting apart before Dr. Y can cut and patch me to a new fragmented wholeness.

Dr. Y hands me a card with her home and office numbers. "Later," she says, "you will think of questions. Call and I'll try to answer them before your surgery next Tuesday morning. Also, when you check into the hospital on Monday afternoon . . ." She stops in midsentence and studies my face as if measuring my need.

She pulls her chair closer and leans toward me. She takes my hand and says, "Believe me, I know what this is like." She places my hand against her right breast and says, "I had surgery three years ago next month."

I am stunned by her confession. I nod, unable to speak in the face of such humanity. I gather my breath in slow waves and take in her words. I whisper the story of Dr. Y's compassion as consolation to myself in the car driving home.

I lie on a gurney outside the operating room on Tuesday morning.

"Tell you my name?" Panic rises from me like a bird. Don't they know my name? As if I could forget my name. I am unable to speak it. I am embarrassed. I cannot remember my name. My body and brain are disconnected from each other.

My thoughts hover over me like a worried parent.

I worry that the hospital could make an error. The surgeon might remove the wrong breast—it's happened before—leaving me with the rogue breast with its offending densities. Then I relax. Congratulate myself for having the foresight to use a marker to leave an arrow and the words *This One* on my rogue breast this morning. And as a nurse prepares me for surgery, she smiles at my note and writes, *Not This One* on my good breast before they give me injections that permit me to float above the soft green lights of the operating table. In the distance, music is piped into overhead speakers. I breathe in time to the music and pray. Masked faces bend over me. Dr. Y and her colleagues have found my carefully labeled breasts. They pull the sheet away; I feel cool air on my abdomen and the room is quiet for a moment. They have found the note I taped to my belly early this morning. The note with questions I could not ask before. I think of questions to add, but it is too late to ask: Will I feel the weight of a phantom breast? Will my grief be bearable?

I said good-bye to a part of me this morning that I realize only now that I love. I long to touch my breast one last time. My arms will not be moved. I feel my breath gather into a cold, unwieldy point. I watch the clock on the wall behind the nurse, but I cannot make sense of time anymore. Is the large hand more important? The clock is faulty. It does not indicate days or years.

A masked face leans over and pats my stomach gently. She injects yellow fluids into the IV in my arm. "Here's your cocktail," says the nurse who holds my hand.

Turning my eyes ever so slightly toward the nurse, I drift away into distant music and lights to a new place. I see a woman wearing a beaded cape; she is performing remarkable feats as she rides a bay pony around a ring. Balancing high above flashing hooves, she stands on one foot at a full canter while the music plays. She looks up and smiles at me.

I believe I've known her all of my life.

AFTER THE RAIN

Maureen had just poured a fresh cup of coffee when she heard Clyde's pickup truck clattering up the driveway. He still had two rusty oil drums rolling around in the back. She opened the curtain over the kitchen sink and watched his truck bounce over the thinly graveled road leading to her house. Her son-in-law wanted something. He never stopped by unless he did. His old truck ground to a halt beside the barn and pebbles pinged underneath the fenders. Dust billowed through the open window and left a gritty taste in her mouth. "Damn you," she grumbled. "No wonder my curtains are filthy.

Clyde slammed his truck door and bounded up the back stairs. On the porch he stomped barn muck off his boots. He yanked open the screen door and called, "Hello. Maureen?" The screen door hinges complained with a throaty squeak.

Maureen flinched as the door banged closed. "One day," she called to him, "you'll rip that door off the hinges." She ran her bent fingers over a folded dish towel. The smell of fresh coffee drew him into the kitchen, like a fly to a screen door.

"Don't need to yell, Maureen." He flashed a broad smile. "I smell something good. You baking cookies?" He licked his thin lips, creased by the sun. He threw his stained cap on the counter and picked up a mug beside the sink. "Man, it's hot. Guess that drought's caught up with us from Texas to Kansas. Farmers got to get some rain. Is this mug clean?" He lifted the pot of fresh coffee and filled the mug. "Weatherman's promised rain for weeks." He opened the refrigerator and leaned on the open door. "Might lose the corn," he said. "Tops turning brown. Damn bad luck."

"You planted too late. This year we've got drought, last year floods."

"What'd you bake today?" he asked. He looked around the kitchen.

She sighed and lifted the aluminum wrap off a plate of sugar cookies on the kitchen table. "Farming's risky business," she said, and pushed the cookies toward him. "Not the best line of work for whiners. Or lazy folks, either."

A whole cookie disappeared into his mouth, leaving a smudge of sugar on his lip. She had hoped May would find a better husband, but May had gotten homesick at college and she'd dropped out after several months and come home. Clyde had been a farmhand for one of their neighbors and was not known for his hard work or good intentions. Fifteen years later there were two rambunctious teenage grandsons, and this son-in-law.

That first afternoon when he'd come to supper, he almost tore the screen door off its hinges, even then, when he opened it. He didn't seem to notice when John said, "Well, Clyde, do you plan to do some door repairs around here?" As he held his fork like a child and gobbled the food, May sat looking pale and frightened.

"He's a clumsy roughneck," Maureen said to John when Clyde had left. She'd had May when she was past forty, after she and John had given up all hope of having children. "We can't let our only child throw away her life on the likes of him." May had always been timid and Maureen couldn't imagine what her daughter saw in such a coarse man. "I can't bear the thought of him."

Maureen was stunned when John sagged into his chair and lowered his head into his hands. "She's run out of choices, as far as I can see. May told me this afternoon. She's two, three months along." Maureen had swallowed her disappointment and tried to like Clyde.

As Clyde drank coffee in greedy gulps, Maureen wondered if she should confront him about the letter she'd gotten about the livestock trailer. "So what do you and May want? Might as well get to the point now; we've had our little weather talk."

Clyde washed the cookie around in his mouth with a swig of coffee and wiped his fingers on his jeans. "Now, Maureen," he said, "what makes you think I want something? Me and May look out for your best interests. You know that."

She frowned. Clyde had borrowed the livestock trailer last month. The next day he called and told her the trailer was wrecked; it was not insured and, fortunately, it was empty. It broke loose, he'd told her on the way home from the livestock auction at Culpeper, and he'd totaled it. "That's the breaks," Clyde had said. "Just write it off on your taxes next year."

She'd thought the trailer was another example of his careless ways. But yesterday she'd gotten a title transfer document from the state motor vehicle office. She called her banker, Frank Black, who told her he'd turned the title lien over to Clyde, since all the paperwork was in good order. He said that Clyde sold the trailer to a man over in Buxton. John had bought that trailer just before he got sick and died. He'd wanted a new one for years.

Maureen scowled as Clyde drummed his fingers on the kitchen table. "Well, that little fender bender in the church parking lot has us wondering if you should be driving." He reached over and patted her hand. "And you don't see as well as you used to . . ." She pulled her hand away and folded her hands in her lap.

"Maureen, old girl, sometimes you're lacking in gratitude."

"Don't call me old girl."

Clyde chuckled. "Sure is hot in this house, Maureen. You need air conditioning. That's the first thing I'd do if it was my house." He waved his hand. "Knock out some walls, too."

"Well, it's not your house. So you can stop talking about knocking out walls." She sighed. "I thought by the time I was seventy-eight, I'd have some peace."

"May and I been thinking maybe you ought to get a place closer to town." He leaned back in his chair. "You're way too old to stay out here by yourself. I'd hate to live alone like this. Aren't you scared?"

"I like the solitude," she said. "Since John died, I cook what I want and eat when I feel like it. I've come to enjoy the peace of summer evenings." She picked up the towel beside the sink. "Most of the time it's quiet."

"Too much wasted space for one person. It's too much for you to keep up."

She studied his face and wished she'd had a son or even another daughter, one with the spine to stand up to someone like Clyde. May did whatever Clyde told her to do.

"We think you should sign over the farm to May. You know, sell it to her for a few token dollars to save everybody from losing out on inheritance taxes. We can get you a room over at Shady Springs. Of course, you'd have a roommate. Costs extra for a private room. But we're willing to chip in on any fees social security and Medicare won't cover." He grinned. "Want to ride over on Sunday and take a look? Place is air-conditioned."

Maureen sat down at the table, folding the dish towel into small squares. Her hands shook. "Where's May in all this? She didn't have the decency to talk with her own mother?" Maureen stood up. She emptied the coffeepot in the sink and turned on the hot water. She wished him out of her kitchen and her house.

"May's busy with the boys today," Clyde said. "We want you thinking about it." He stood up. "Look, just between you and me, old girl, you got to do this sooner or later. You got nobody but us in this world, so you might as well get on with it. We need to do this before you fall and break a hip or something."

"No, Clyde, I'm not moving to any old folks' home. I'm healthy, and not daft, yet."

"Of course, another option is for May, the boys, and me to go ahead and move in here with you, preferably before winter. The boys need their own rooms now that they're getting older. It makes a lot of sense. You can move into the small bedroom behind the kitchen." He stared at the worn linoleum floor. "Like I told May, you don't need much space." He stood at the kitchen doorway and looked at her intently. "Be good if we could take care of this before your birthday next month. Either way, we'd get you settled in by the end of summer." He rubbed his hands together. "You can still cook and have your garden, and May could get a full-time job." He turned to leave. "I'd make a better go of this farm than John."

"Not yet, Clyde. Go on home and leave me alone." She held the door open.

She stood at the door as the truck plunged through swirling dust down the driveway to the highway.

She'd forgotten to mention the livestock trailer. Clyde had forged her signature on the papers. That much was certain. She could prove it, but then what? Maureen went into the bathroom off the kitchen and washed her face. She stared at her reflection in the mirror. The old woman in the mirror was afraid. She had always depended on John. He'd sheltered her from details, probably too much. He'd never wanted her to be too independent, but he'd been sweet about it. He'd watched the news and said women's liberation was a crazy idea cooked up by some lonely woman who needed a good man. Early in their marriage Maureen had learned to avoid disagreements with her husband, but sometimes she felt guilty that she'd not stood up to him more often and told him her own opinions. She had wondered if it was partly her fault May couldn't adjust to college and was so weak.

Maureen leaned on the narrow bathroom windowsill and looked into her backyard. She couldn't imagine leaving her home. She feared leaving more than dying. A couple of old speckled hens pecked at patches of grass. Her garden stretched beyond, marked by wooden tomato stakes and tired beanstalks. As a young woman, she had felt a surge of pride over the baskets of tomatoes, beans, and peppers she had grown, cooked, and canned on busy summer afternoons while John worked on the tractor. The pleasure of biting into ripe, sweet tomatoes, warm and fragrant from the sun left her dizzy, even now, just thinking about it.

The bathroom was stuffy. Maureen tried to open the window, but it was stuck. As she forced the window open, arthritis pains throbbed in her fingers. She shook her hands and pressed them to her temples. When she grasped the plastic curtain to tie it away from the window, it cracked and crumbled in her palm. She wiped her hands on her dress. She would deal with Clyde. She would drive into town and talk to Sam Brewer, John's old attorney. Maybe he could help her, before it was too late. She would tell him about the trailer, too.

The afternoon was hot and breezy. Although the sun was strong overhead, dark clouds drifted along the horizon and the smell of rain hung in the air. Off in the distance locusts sang near the pond. Maureen opened her mouth and tasted the air, aware of the coming change. Summer rains teased the senses. Since childhood, she'd loved the keen shifts in the air, a subtle change in the clicks of summer locusts before a rain.

Maureen smoothed her dress and combed her short gray hair. She moved decisively into dim light in her bedroom, where curtains kept out the afternoon glare. Usually she took a nap during the heat of the day but not today. She fumbled in a dresser drawer for her keys, plucked up her favorite purple hat she'd crocheted years earlier from a magazine pattern. "For luck," Maureen said. She grasped the hat and locked her door.

She had no choice but to drive John's old Chevy truck. Her car was still in the shop for repairs. The garage had ordered new bumper and fender panels to repair the damage from her accident.

As Maureen swung open the doors to the wooden car shed behind her house, dust motes danced in a beam of sunshine that fell across the hood. Cloaked in cobwebs, the truck seemed captured by brown fuzzy-legged spiders that hung from the rafters. She cleaned the door off with a broom and climbed behind the wheel. She stretched her feet to the gas pedal and groped for the handle to pull the seat closer to the wheel. Since John's death, she rarely drove his truck. Old Spice and perspiration lingered in the cab and stung her eyes. Even now she had images of his square tanned hands on the steering wheel and that unruly lock of hair over his right ear. He'd teased her for being a homebody, but she'd never really liked to travel, even to town.

For years John had driven the ten miles to town once each week. He bought supplies, seed, and tractor parts, and stayed all afternoon talking with friends at Thompson's Feed Store, but he was a homebody, too. Reluctantly, he'd taught her to drive after she was past sixty, when she had insisted on learning. He guided her with soothing words. She'd gained confidence as she shifted gears and lurched down the driveway, until she was competent enough to pass the driver's test.

While he was alive she drove them both to church on Sundays just to practice driving. He was amused at being driven, but after his heart attack and then a stroke left him shriveled and sick, Maureen knew she'd done the right thing to learn to drive.

Last month after the accident May had insisted on driving Maureen while her car was in the shop. Now she stopped by on Sunday mornings driving her to church, and into town on Wednesdays for the few groceries she needed. She had urged her mother to give up her driver's license. "But, Ma, you're too old to drive. I worry about your shifting gears with your arthritis, and you don't look behind you when you back up. I'm afraid you'll hurt somebody."

Maureen turned the key and the engine coughed and started. She noticed that Clyde had left the window open on the passenger side when he'd borrowed it last month. She eased the truck over the gravel driveway and swung a hard right turn onto the highway.

As the truck gained speed, she switched on the radio and searched for a station with music. She glanced up just in time to see a pheasant swoop inches from the windshield, startling her. She slammed on the brakes. A screwdriver and a plastic cup rolled from under the seat against her feet.

Shaken, she eased the truck over to the edge of the road and lifted her hand to her face. She thought of turning around and going home, but she couldn't turn back now. She pulled onto the road and drove slowly. As she passed the Shady Springs Retirement Center, she looked at the white, sterile building. Years ago when the building was under construction, John had said, "Not much of a place to live, but it's better than no home at all for poor souls without family. I don't ever want either of us to end in a place like that."

Clouds rolled across the horizon like tumbleweeds. She drove the remaining miles to town and parked under an oak tree near the courthouse. An old woman sat on a bench across the street. Two black plastic bags lay at her feet. Maureen didn't recognize her, and it occurred to her that the woman might be homeless. Thunder rumbled in the blackening sky and Maureen's sense of unease grew. Perhaps she should have called Sam instead of driving into town.

Sam Brewer's office was on the second floor of a faded three-story brick building beside the courthouse. She gripped the handrail and pulled herself up the narrow stairs leading to Sam's office, pausing at the landings, disoriented by the dim light. Medicinal odors from the dentist's office on the third floor hung in the air, and the whine of a dental drill echoed in the hallway. She stopped to catch her breath before she opened the frosted glass door.

Sam had been John's lawyer for years. His hands always felt damp, and when she'd told John, he'd laughed. "Women," he said, shaking his head. "Funny, the things you notice."

Maureen had not been to Sam's office since she'd settled John's estate. But thanks to John's careful planning, there was enough money to let her keep the farm. Although Clyde had urged her to sell off some of the land, John's arrangements provided for her with money from leasing the fields. Clyde's disappointment was clear. He had counted on adding John's farm to his own small acreage.

"Maureen Cordell. How are you?" Sam said, standing up at his cluttered desk, smoothing his thin red hair. His tan shirt sleeves were rolled up, the collar unbuttoned. A wrinkled green tie hung loosely knotted at his throat. He worked alone now that his secretary had died.

He grasped her hand. "Great to see you. Clyde called me last week and said you might stop by."

She leaned over and set her pocketbook on the floor, discreetly wiping her hand on her skirt.

Sam pulled two chairs close together facing each other. "Sit here," he said, touching the closest one. "Can I get you some water? Fountain in the hall broke a while back," Sam said as he filled a paper cup with water from a jug on his desk. "Dry as a politician's speech out there on the farms, but it sure looks like rain today. We can always hope for a bit of rain." He handed her the cup. "Now what can I do for you today?"

"Yes," she said. "Thanks." She sipped the water and set the cup down on his desk. "I came to get advice," she said, as a hard cold place formed in her stomach. She had not known she would drive into town to see Sam until an hour ago. But clearly he seemed to be expecting her.

"I understand you're thinking of signing everything over to your family," Sam said, smiling. "Avoid those pesky inheritance taxes, I always say. Clyde told me you're thinking of moving into Shady Springs." He poured himself a cup of water. "Good to get you in a place with folks your age. Best thing you could do."

"No, Sam, I'm not looking to move." She swallowed hard. "I'd appreciate it if you didn't refer to Clyde like he was my own flesh and blood." Her stomach churned at the thought of Clyde plotting.

"Okay, Maureen, why don't you tell me what's on your mind?"

"Can anyone make me leave my home?" Her voice shook. "Can they force me out?"

"Well, I guess it depends on whether your family feels like you're competent. Whether you can take care of yourself." He cleared his throat. "Sometimes these decisions become questions for the courts to decide, but that rarely happens. Do you feel you can take care of yourself? If you need to have someone around to help, maybe Clyde, May, and the boys should move in with you."

"No. I'm healthy. I've got my wits about me, Sam. I know what's going on."

She picked up her pocketbook and held it in her lap. "I know Clyde took John's livestock trailer, forged signatures on the papers, and sold it. I want to press charges. I found out Clyde sold it to a man over in Buxton."

"Goodness me. Those are serious charges to make against a family member." Sam cleared his throat. "Perhaps this is a family matter, not a problem for the courts, if you all can just sit down and talk."

"Get a handwriting expert to examine everything." She heard her voice grow shrill. "You'll see."

"You got a lot of arthritis in your hands. You know how unsteady your handwriting was back when we settled the papers on John's estate." He smiled evenly, his thin lips stretching over his teeth. "Can't say you had much use for that old trailer." He shifted in his chair and chuckled. "You planning to take up hauling livestock?"

She tightened her grip on her pocketbook. "It was almost new."

"Sometimes when people get older, they mix things up in their mind. Get confused. Maybe you signed those papers? Maybe you just forgot. Clyde and May are looking out for you as best they can. And of course they're worried about your driving. He seems like a straightforward fellow to me. He says you're getting a little forgetful these days."

When she failed to speak, Sam folded his arms and leaned forward. "Clyde and May are all the family you got. They will inherit everything eventually, so I don't see why this matters." Sam pulled his chair closer and patted her on the arm. "Everybody's looking after you, like we promised John. Now if, for example, you weren't living alone in that old house . . ." Sam smiled and leaned closer. "You know, they worry about you. Why what if you fell? And people your age sometimes walk off and forget they've left a pot going on the stove. Why, I've even done that myself and I'm a bit younger than you are, but the point is they do worry."

"You never treated John like a child," she said, "even when he was so sick at the end." Anger rose in her throat. She grasped the arms of her chair and stood up. "Sorry to trouble you," she said. "I guess it is a family matter."

Sam smiled gently. "Easy there, Maureen, don't get upset." Rain pelted the windows. "Well, we're finally getting that much-needed rain," he said. The lamp on his desk flickered. "Course the power will likely go off any minute now." His features softened and he reached out his hand to her.

"Your family's looking out for you, Maureen." A crack of thunder rattled the windows. "Don't leave now. Wait until this storm blows over." He glanced out the window. "Want me to draw up the papers for you to look over? Seriously, I hate to see John's hard-earned money go to taxes."

"No, Sam, not yet." She moved toward the door. "I worked hard for it too."

He sighed. "I wish you'd at least wait until it stops raining." He called after her, "You're mighty lucky you've got family. I wish me and Lucy had a couple of kids."

Maureen gripped the handrail on the stairs until her hands ached. She threw open the door and stepped outside into the storm as heavy rains washed over the building. Rain stung her face and arms, reminding her of all the times she'd rushed outside to bring laundry in from the clothesline, wind and rain whipping sheets and towels against her face. She hurried to the truck, wrenched open the heavy door, and sat behind the wheel gasping. She was soaked to the skin; her cotton dress clung to her. Water dripped off her hat. So much for luck, she thought. She pulled it off and wrung water onto the floor of the truck.

She wiped her face and started the truck. Driving slowly along Main Street, she passed the town's only bus stop. The old woman she'd seen earlier stood huddled against the back wall of the bus shelter that was covered with billboards for cigarettes and shampoo. Two black plastic bags lay at her feet. "Homeless," Maureen muttered. Jolted by the word, she swallowed the metallic edge of fear that crept into her mouth as she drove past. The woman wore a pink knitted cloche hat, like hers. The forlorn hat tilted precariously on her head. Maureen drove around the block and pulled up in front of the shelter. The windshield wipers clip-clopped back and forth as she leaned out the window and looked at the woman. "Hello," she said.

The woman was tall, thin, and hungry looking. She pushed wispy gray hair under her hat and nodded. "If you're going to ask me for directions," she said, "I can't tell you a thing about this town. I never lived around here. I used to live over in Downey." She wiped the rain from her face.

"Get in," Maureen said, surprised at her own behavior, "before you catch your death."

"Oh, I shouldn't. You see, I got these bundles," the woman said. "I'd hate to get your truck wet." She looked at Maureen cautiously. "My goodness," she said, "why, you're wetter than I am."

"Put them here on the floor or throw them in the back of the truck," Maureen said. Thunder rumbled. "Hurry, looks like this storm is picking up steam again." *What have I done?* Maureen thought as the old woman lifted her bags into the truck. Rain blew in the open door and the woman settled into the seat beside her.

"This is kind of you," said the woman. "I'm Sophie Bickel."

"Maureen Cordell. Now where can I take you?"

"Well, I don't really know." Sophie sniffed and wiped her face with a handkerchief. "Maybe I'll just ride with you a ways until this storm clears. I used my last few dollars on a bus ticket to Buxton to see my cousin, Lucille Morley. But when I got there yesterday, I found out she was dead. Died about a year ago."

"That's too bad," Maureen said. "Where did you stay last night?"

"Slept in a barn down behind an Amoco gas station," Sophie said.

Maureen stared in amazement. "Oh my. How terrible!" She couldn't imagine sleeping in a barn.

"It was a shock," Sophie said, "my last living relative pushing up grass. Nobody bothered to tell me she'd gone to a nursing home. Last time I had a letter a few years ago, she was fine."

"Don't think I know anybody over in Buxton," Maureen said, "but then the town's grown since they built that new chemical plant."

Sophie removed her wet hat and ran her fingers through her hair. "Oh dear, I look a fright. Everything I own is soaking wet and dirty in those trash bags. Surprised you'd pick me up, looking frowsy, like I do. I smell like a wet dog. I'm not usually dirty, but this has been a rough week."

Maureen glanced at the woman. "Come on out to my house. We'll both get cleaned up and find dry clothes. Looks like you and I wear about the same size. I live on a farm ten miles down the highway."

"That's good of you, but I don't want to trouble you. Lots of people are afraid of someone like me. I can't quite think of myself as homeless, although it must be so, but I haven't always lived this way."

The woman must've been at least seventy, though maybe she was younger. Her skin looked weathered, but her blue eyes twinkled like they knew a secret or two.

"I lived in Downey before I lost my house in that flood last summer. Couldn't afford flood insurance on my pension." She chuckled. "Never expected to spend my golden years hitchhiking."

Maureen nodded. "That was a terrible flood. Our church sent food and clothes."

Sophie smiled. "It helped, but it's no way to live. This homeless business has been an education. Local people from the churches helped for a couple of weeks, but sermons about how floods were the Lord's will got on my nerves."

Maureen tried to imagine it. "To start over so late in life, makes me sad to think about it."

"I can't tell you how I ache for the way things were. I stayed for a while in one of those shelters, but I had no privacy at all. Couldn't pass gas without everyone knowing my business."

Maureen chuckled.

"And I found out people will steal from you, even when you carry all you own in a bag. It taught me to look at people a whole new way." Sophie propped her feet on one of the bags on the floor. "I always thought this homeless stuff happened to people who were losers, not someone like me. I've learned to rethink just about everything now that I don't spend my days watching television. Why I'm living my drama, honey, and I'll never need to see a TV again."

"How in the world have you managed to live?" Maureen asked. She didn't think she would survive sleeping on the ground in terrible places. Her back ached if she even sat too long watching television.

"It has been hard," Sophie said. "But I found out how little I need."

"Look. The sky's clearing up a bit over toward the east where we're headed," Maureen said. "The clouds are floating higher now."

"I used to love to watch the weather channel. Look at those cumulus clouds! What in the world were you doing out in a storm like this?"

"Went to see my lawyer," Maureen said. "But I wasted my time."

"Don't have no use for lawyers myself," Sophie said.

"My daughter, May, and my no-good son-in-law are out to get their hands on my farm. Guess they're not even willing to wait until I die." She hadn't really said how she felt about this to anyone before. For a moment the hurt and disappointment almost choked her.

"That's too bad. I always wished I'd had children," Sophie said. "A daughter would've been nice."

"Not if you'd had one like mine. I don't know what's the matter with her. She's just so weak. I wish she had more backbone."

Maureen turned the truck into the drive. "Well. Here we are." Already winds were drying the corn growing in the leased fields around her house. She drove the truck into the shed and set the parking brake. "Were you ever married?"

"My Hayward died in a truck accident five years ago this October." She patted a white plastic bag in her lap. "I keep some of his things here. I like having his old work shirt and shaving mug."

Maureen glanced at the bag. She kept John's shaving mug in her bedside table, and some of his clothes still hung in their closet. She'd given his suit and a few dress shirts to charity.

"I had Hayward's ashes in a silver box, but some creep stole it at the shelter." Her eyes filled. "You know when I decided to marry him, I looked up the meaning of his name. *Hayward* means 'guardian of the forest.'" She smiled. "After that I knew I'd be safe with him. He was so kind to everyone he ever met."

"Come on," Maureen said, "I'll help you get these bags into the house. We'll get into dry clothes and start a big load of wash going."

Once in the house, Maureen put on a fresh pot of coffee. "I'll lay out a couple of outfits and some shoes for you to try," she said. "They'll be on the bed in the spare bedroom just down the hall."

While Sophie went to take a shower, Maureen started a load of laundry. She unwrapped the sugar cookies and placed them in the middle of her kitchen table. She hummed to herself as she set out her best cups and saucers and stood back to admire the pretty arrangement on the table.

Sophie walked into the kitchen. "That shower was perfect. Hope you don't mind that I used your hairdryer. That coffee smells wonderful." Sophie looked at the table and smiled. "I know people matter more than things, but it's awful to lose things that hold memories. My good dishes were lost in the flood. I love this pattern."

"How nice to set the table and have someone appreciate it." Maureen said. "That dress fits like it was made for you."

"Thank you." Sophie smiled. "I feel more like a human being again." She picked up Maureen's purple hat from the kitchen chair. "You've got a hat like mine, only mine is pink. I noticed it in the truck, but I forgot to say anything." She examined it. "It sure is wet. But these are nice stitches. I worked a needlepoint row of rosebuds around the band on mine. Held the string tight like this and formed French knots." She sewed the stitches in the air with her hands.

"Was that pattern in a *Family Circle* magazine a few years back?" Maureen asked.

"Why, yes it was. That same magazine always ran a recipe for a no-egg pound cake a couple of times every year. Did you ever try it?"

"You baked one, too?" Maureen said. "Well, my cake turned out awful. I fed it to the chickens."

"And mine tasted okay, but Hayward didn't like it. He said a good cake needs eggs and I agree." Sophie picked up her wet hat. "Just look at this. I'm afraid the rain's ruined both our hats."

"Oh, it's not too ruined," Maureen said, picking up Sophie's hat. "Bet if we washed these in a dab of liquid dish soap and stretched them over one of those round globe lights, they'd dry out almost good as new."

As they sat in the kitchen and talked, Maureen wondered what it would be like to have someone share the house with her, help her with the garden. She'd never considered it until now. She wondered if Sophie knew how to drive.

Sophie sipped her coffee and sighed. "It's so peaceful here. You're lucky."

They could plant late vegetables, Maureen thought. There was still a little time before first frost. She glanced outside. The sunset gave off a peach glow. "In the summer after a big storm we have these grand evenings up here on this hill."

"Have you ever noticed how clean the air is after rain?" Sophie said. "It clears my head."

"What do you think we ought to cook for supper?" Maureen asked. "I'm getting hungry and I know you must be too." She stood up and opened the refrigerator. "How about if I scrambled some eggs and sliced this wonderful smoked ham? Oh, and I have a loaf of fresh bread I baked early this morning. And I have a real pound cake made with eggs that's good, if I do say so myself."

Sophie smiled. "That sounds wonderful," she said. "Got any pickled tomato relish?"

"Yes, indeed," Maureen said. "I put them up myself, but I'll need help getting the jars opened." She held up her hands. Opening and closing her fingers slowly, she said, "Just a bit of arthritis."

The phone rang, a shrill interruption that echoed in the kitchen.

Maureen answered the phone and heard May's nasal whine. "Ma? Where have you been? I tried to call you twice during that storm." May's television blared in the background.

Maureen pictured Clyde parked in his recliner in his underwear drinking a tall beer and watching the crop reports on Channel 11.

"I hope you weren't outside in that terrible rain. Were you asleep or what? When you didn't answer my calls, I feared for the worst. I was about to send one of the boys to check on you."

"Well, May, don't worry. I'm fine, but I don't have time to talk right now. I've got an old friend from out of town visiting me. We're about to sit down to eat." She smiled at Sophie. "But don't worry. We'll talk tomorrow, May."

Acknowledgments
Flight Path & Other Stories

Many of these stories were published previously, and nominated for awards; several have been reimagined and retitled:

"Mermaids"—won the 2011 Roanoke Review Prize for Fiction, published in *Roanoke Review 2012*, vol. xxxvii, September 2012. Nominated for a Pushcart Prize and Best American Short Stories.

"Flight Path" ---has been extensively revised for this collection. A previous version under the title "Flight"—was a Glimmer Train Honorable-Mention for the November 2012 Short Story Award for New Writers and a finalist for the *2013 Rash Award* for fiction by *Broad River Review* and short listed for the *2014 Phoebe Fiction Award* and the *Folio Fiction Contest*.

"Rabbits"— published in *Uncertain Promise: An Anthology of Short Fiction and Creative Nonfiction*. Edited by Von Pittman. October 2014. And named a 2013 finalist in the Phoebe Fiction Contest.

"After the Rain"—published in *Big Muddy*, vol. 11, no. 2, April 2012.

"This Arrow Marks Me"—published in *The Broadkill Review*, vol. 5, no. 5, September/October 2011. Nominated for a Pushcart Prize 2011. Previously named a finalist in the *2011 "So-to-Speak" Contest* under the title of *Four Tuesdays*.

"Kindness"—published in *Evening Street Review*, Issue 12, May 2015.

"Skating Blind"—published in *Buffalo Spree*, Winter 1997. Nominated for Best American Short Stories and O. Henry Award.

"Wait on Me"—published as "Pancakes" in *Minimus*, vol. 7, 1997. (revised)

"Unnatural Disaster"—published in *Folio: A Literary Journal*, Winter 1995.

The author acknowledges the encouragement of family, friends, and colleagues from Tinker Mountain Workshops and The Gettysburg Writers Workshops for their wise advice. A special thanks goes to Fred Leebron, Daniel J. Mueller, Pinckney Benedict and Lee K. Abbott who encouraged this work. Thanks to Ally Machate and Harrison Demchick http://www.thewritersally.com for editing assistance on this project. Also I am so grateful to Elizabeth McCracken who believed I could do it.